Tea for Two

The Bella Novella Collection, Book Two

By

Janice Thompson

Tea for Two
© 2016 by Janice Thompson

Scripture references are from The Holy Bible, New International Version®, niv®. Copyright © 1973, 1978, 1984 by International Bible Society. Used by permission of Zondervan.

All characters are fictional. Any resemblances to actual people or events are purely coincidental.

Dedication

To Penelope Marie.
Every little princess deserves a tea party welcome!

Table of Contents

Blessed is the nation whose God is the Lord, the people whom he has chosen as his heritage!
Psalm 22:12 ESV

CHAPTER ONE
Love Will Keep Us Together

It has been said that politics is the second oldest profession. I have learned that it bears a striking resemblance to the first.
Ronald Reagan

There are some holidays that just put a smile on your face. Take Valentine's Day, for instance. I was always a fan, even before I met my sweetie, D.J. The dreamer in me always believed in Cupid's arrows and happily ever afters. Of course, the truest "forever" love stories didn't always start in such a fanciful way. But Valentine's Day awakened the dreamer in me. Blame it on the wedding business.

People always fought to get their weddings scheduled at Club Wed on Valentine's Day weekend. Sometimes we would host up to four weddings in a two day period. This year we only had two: a smallish Saturday the 13th event for a couple in their golden years, and the big one, a full-out Valentine's Day tea party themed soiree on Sunday afternoon. On that day Victoria Felicity Brierley—of the Houston Brierleys—was scheduled to marry longtime Texas senator, Beaurgard—aka "Beau"—DeVine, of the Dallas-area DeVines. To complicate matters, the bride's family insisted she keep all of her names. On the day she married, she would become Mrs. Victoria Felicity Brierley-DeVine. Quite a mouthful, especially for a woman with a husband in politics. No doubt the talking heads would have a doozie of a time with this one.

None of that mattered to me, however. I simply wanted to comply with the bride's wishes to have the day of her dreams. And that's exactly what I planned to give her—a Victorian tea party, with all of the frills one would expect at such an event. I had to wonder if Beauregard would balk at the idea of a tea party theme, but it turned out the kindly fellow was an ultra-conservative with true Tea Party leanings. He planned to use the theme to his political advantage. He didn't seem to mind the wedding's theme, even after the bride explained that he would have to wear a turn-of-the-century suit and sip hot tea from a porcelain cup with flowers painted on it. Turned out, Mr.

DeVine simply wanted to make the future Mrs. DeVine happy and for that I had to give him props.

Planning for a Valentine's celebration was nothing new. I'd hosted tons of weddings, after all. But, in all my years of putting together themed weddings, I'd never hosted one that involved Victorian gowns, porcelain teapots, hundreds of teacups and imported lace tablecloths, valued at over two hundred dollars apiece.

On the morning of January 11th, a text came through on my phone with a picture attached. Wowza. I'd seen a lot of wedding gowns in my day, but this one looked like it came straight off of the Titanic. I could almost envision Jack and Rose strolling across the first class deck now, arm in arm. Talk about all things vintage and lace. I'd never seen so much of it, in fact. Seconds later, my phone rang. I smiled when I saw the bride's name on the screen.

"Victoria?"

"Yes, Bella." She let out a little giggle. "It's me."

"Great gown, girl! Wow. I've never seen anything like it."

"Thanks. Just picked it up from the alterations lady. I'm in love. I thought I'd send you the picture so you'd have a better idea about the style of lace I've been talking about." She paused and then added, "Hey, how was your cruise?"

"Our cruise?" I spoke the words and sighed. "D.J. and I had the best time ever. I missed the kids, of course, but we video-chatted nearly every day. Mama and Rosa saw to that."

"You saw the Eiffel tower?"

"We saw everything from Santorini to Spain. But not the Eiffel tower. That's in Paris. We didn't make it that far."

"Oh, right." She laughed. "Silly me. I'm so distracted, Bella. I can't sleep, I can't eat, I can't . . ." She paused. "What was I saying? Oh yes, I can't remember what I was saying. Or doing. Is this normal?"

"Four and a half weeks before your wedding day? I'd say."

"Well, good, because I was starting to feel like an anomaly. I'm not the typical bride, I know. I mean, how many of your brides travel in political circles?"

"Not many, I have to confess. You're my first, in fact. And just for the record, I'm still jet-lagged, so I'm pretty out of it too. We just got back yesterday. Haven't caught up to Galveston time yet. And my body still thinks we're on the ship, so everything's wobbly."

"Oh, sorry. You okay to talk or should I call back later?"

"Totally fine." I did my best to stifle the yawn that tried to sneak out. "What's up?"

"Well, here's the deal. Beau-Beau is running for president, as you know."

"Wait. . ." I paused, thinking I'd heard incorrectly. "President of the United States?"

"Well, of course, silly. You didn't think I meant president of his fraternity, did you? Anyway, he's running for president and he's gaining momentum."

"When did this happen?" I scratched my head, completely discombobulated by this news. "I mean, I know he's a senator and all, but. . .president? Like, president, president?"

"Where have you been, Bella? Didn't you watch the last debate? Beauregard is doing very well with conservative voters. He's got quite a fan base."

"Debate?" I hardly found time to watch my favorite TV shows, let alone political debates. And everyone in town knew the Rossis kept their political beliefs to themselves. Well, all but Rosa, who let her passion for Jimmy Carter slip during a recent episode of *The Italian Kitchen*.

"Right. Anyway, Beau is soaring upward in the polls. I don't want to alarm you, Bella, but this means the wedding will require top-notch security. Have you ever had the Secret Service at one of your ceremonies?"

"Secret Service? The guys in black suits and sunglasses? No. We've never had Secret Service at one of our weddings. When Brock Benson came we had body guards, but they didn't wear sunglasses."

"Then this will be a first. And I can't believe you got to meet Brock Benson in person." She let out a little squeal. "Lucky you!"

"We're good friends. You know they filmed several episodes of his show on the island, right? But let's go back to talking about your wedding. You're saying it's going to be high-level security because Beau is running for. . .president?"

"Yes, and we'll have to work our schedule carefully. There are a couple more debates between now and the wedding day. In fact, there's one on the night of the 13th of February."

"February 13th?" The night before her wedding? Really?

"Are you saying we'll have to reschedule the rehearsal?" I asked. "Because that weekend is going to be pretty crazy already. We got a small wedding on Saturday, the 13th. I can't change that."

"No, no. Wouldn't matter if we moved the rehearsal to another date. . .he still wouldn't be there. Things are going to be crazy that week."

I wanted to ask the obvious: *Do you think you guys should just wait until after the election?* But I didn't want to get into her business. Not that she let me get a word in edgewise.

"The thing is, Bella, I'm going to be really, really busy. We've got the campaign trail, debates, the Iowa Caucus, and then the New Hampshire primary. And Beau's got to be on-point every step of the way, which means—"

"That you're in charge of the wedding plans?" I tried. "Don't worry about that. I've coordinated a ton of weddings where the bride did most of the planning without the groom's direct involvement. Lots of guys just go along with whatever you think, anyway."

"No, that's not what I meant at all. The whole tea party theme, well, it's as much his as mine. What I'm trying to say, Bella, is that I'm really going to depend on you artistically. I won't have time to think through the finer details of what the cake should look like, what the décor should be. . .all of that. I have some ideas, for sure, and I'll share them with you. But I want to give you full leeway to take the ball and run with it. I've heard so much about you from Justine and I saw her wedding first-hand back in December. What a night! It was spectacular."

"Still can't get over the fact that it actually snowed the night of a meteorologist's wedding, can you?" I laughed.

"Right? But my point is, I feel like I know you because I've seen your work. You'll pull this off Bella. And I want you to know that money is no object. Beau will see to that. This is going to be a grand event. So, don't feel limited by finances. We've got that part covered."

"Great. That certainly makes things easier. And I don't mind taking care of the finer points, but I want to make sure I've got the theme right. Tea party. Old-fashioned."

"Right." She hollered something to someone on her end and then returned to the phone. "Sorry about that. Now, I know we can't do an outdoor wedding in February, but I want the whole thing to have that sort of feel. Quaint. Charming. Vintage. You know. Like a true afternoon tea in the garden—only inside. At night."

"I see."

I'd never really done a tea party themed wedding before, but how hard could it be, really? Vintage lace tablecloths with a two hundred dollar pricetag. At least she'd already taken care of that. Pretty dishes. I'd have to locate some that looked like they came from the turn of the century. An elegant cake. . .and voila! Surely the Rossis could pull this off. I hoped.

Another yawn escaped and Victoria laughed. "Okay, okay, I can take the hint. You go back to sleep, Bella. Let your body catch up to Texas time. We can talk later, once the jetlag has passed. I need to get back to Beau-Beau anyway. He has a television interview in an hour and he's hopeless without me at his side. You know how men are."

Actually, I knew nothing of hopeless men. Most of the guys in my life were the hard-working, self-sufficient type. Okay, all but Pop, who depended on Mama for pretty much everything. But luckily he wasn't running for president of the United States.

Beau DeVine was, though. . .and that pretty much changed everything about the upcoming Valentine's wedding. I'd better get all of my ducks in a row. . .and then pray they weren't shot down by some random Secret Service guy. Heavens! Did I ever have my work cut out for me!

CHAPTER TWO
To Know Him is to Love Him

Man is by nature a political animal.
Aristotle

A couple of days after Victoria's call, Mama popped her head in my office and whispered, "The men in suits are here. . .and they're asking for you."

"Men in suits?" I looked up from my work, intrigued by her words. "Huh?"

"Secret Service." Her eyes widened and she took a couple of steps inside the room. "And no, I'm not kidding. Not even close."

I rose, and my hands began to tremble. "Secret Service? Like, the Secret Service, Secret Service?"

"The real deal. They're at the front door. If Rosa hadn't been cleaning out Guido's cage, we wouldn't have noticed them." Mama's voice quivered and she lowered it to a whisper. "But it's kind of hard to miss a bunch of guys in black suits wearing sunglasses at nine in the morning, you know?"

"Well, yes. . .but, Secret Service? Don't they usually fly under the radar? Why would they tell you who they are?"

None of this made sense. Wouldn't Victoria have warned me the Secret Service guys were on their way today? A girl should have a heads-up for something that important.

I rose and smoothed the wrinkles out of my blouse, then gave my appearance a glance in the mirror. Hmm. I needed to touch up my lipstick, but maybe they wouldn't mind that.

I followed Mama into the front hallway and my breath caught in my throat when I saw six—no, seven—men in black suits standing there. Maybe she'd misunderstood. Maybe these guys were funeral directors, lost on their way to a convention or something.

"Bella Neeley?" The one closest to me pulled off his sunglasses, revealing bight blue eyes. "I'm Agent O'Conner, with the Secret Service."

Okay, then. . .not a funeral convention.

"I'm Bella Neeley." The words came out a bit squeaky. Probably nerves. "How can I help you?"

"We're here to scope out the place before the DeVine wedding. You'll be seeing us come and go over the next few weeks. We need top security clearance due to the current political climate. I'm sure you understand."

"Oh, Club Wed is perfectly safe," I said. "We've never had an incident here." I paused and my nose wrinkled. "Well, unless you count the time my Uncle Laz caught Bubba's eyebrows on fire. But that was totally an accident. Accidents happen." I offered a strained smile.

Agent O'Conner pulled out a notepad and scribbled something down. "Who is this Uncle Laz? Is he currently on the premises or was he incarcerated after the incident?"

"Oh, no sir, not incarcerated. He's free as a bird. He and Aunt Rosa just got back from Italy a few weeks ago. They had a terrific second honeymoon. Speaking of which, my husband and I just arrived home from a Mediterranean cruise a couple of weeks ago, ourselves."

"You've been traveling in the Middle East?" Agent O'Conner quirked a brow. "What was the nature of your visit?"

"The nature of it? Like I said, it was a second honeymoon. D.J. and I—D.J. is my husband—anyway, D.J. and I went to Santorini, Italy, and Spain. Oh, and Turkey. We were supposed to get off in Turkey but with the current unrest, well, you know. We had to stay on the ship."

"This D.J. fellow—will he be at the wedding?"

"Oh, sure. He'll be running sound."

"We'll need to clear the sound equipment," O'Conner said. "In fact, we'll need to clear every square inch of this place. I hope you realize the seriousness of this process, Mrs. Neeley."

"I do." Sort of. Until five minutes ago I had pretty much thought of the DeVine wedding as a fairly typical event. That had certainly changed.

"Just so you understand, Mrs. Neeley, our assignment here will include setting up security posts, making inspections, providing safety and/or emergency response, if necessary. We will service the facilities and surrounding areas on the night of the wedding by monitoring and operating various pieces of communications equipment, along with other advanced technologies that will help us detect and/or identify high-risk items or people. We are also authorized to make arrests. Do you have any questions?"

Um, yeah. I had about ten, but couldn't seem to remember them right now. And my heart was suddenly *thump-thumping* so loudly I couldn't hear anything the man said.

"You're here to protect the bride?" I asked, my voice probably too loud. "Or the groom?"

"Technically, Title 18 U.S.C. 2056a7 authorizes the U.S. Secret Service to protect spouses of major presidential and vice presidential candidates within 120 days of the general presidential election. As the election is not for several months, the time frame does not fall within those boundaries. So, to answer your question, we are here to protect the groom."

"You're saying the bride's on her own?" I offered what came out sounding like a weak laugh.

"Do we have reason to be concerned about her well-being, Mrs. Neeley?" He gave me a penetrating gaze.

"Heavens, no. I'm just making light conversation."

"We don't make light conversation."

Okay then.

"And just for the record, the wedding locale is top secret. Even the guests won't know the location until the day of the ceremony. We expect your full cooperation in keeping this event on the down-low."

"But the vendors. . .won't they have to know?"

"The ones who need to know will know." He gave me a stern look. "Got it?"

"Um, got it."

We spent the next hour and a half going over every square inch of Club Wed. So much for getting my work done this morning. Who were these guys, to think they could just show up unannounced and interrupt my workday? Oh yeah. They were the Secret Service. And I'd better do everything they demanded.

After going over the building with a fine-toothed comb, one of them—the tallest fellow in the dark suit—pulled out a small camera and began to take pictures.

"I wish I'd known you were coming," I said. "The room is filled with stuff I brought back from the Middle East."

"Middle East?" He turned to face me, his eyes narrowing to slits. "Could you elaborate?"

"Yes. I'd be happy to elaborate. We went on a cruise and I found the most gorgeous items. Thought they'd be perfect for centerpieces. Want to see them?"

"I want to see everything you brought home from the Middle East, but first I have a question: Did you meet any strangers?"

"Oh, lots of strangers. There was this great guy we met on the ship. . .his name was Abdul Something-or-Another. We really liked him a lot. He and his wife live in Egypt. Or maybe it was Kenya. Is it terrible that I can't remember?"

"Did this Abdul Something-or-Another give you any packages, Mrs. Neeley?"

"No. Nothing. Just a lot of great conversation."

"Mm-hmm." He continued snapping photos, then turned his camera on me. I wasn't sure if I should pose or give him a mug-shot face.

I opted for the "What do you think you're doing taking my picture without asking?" pose.

He didn't seem to notice or care.

"Okay, Mrs. Rossi, we need to see your identification."

"It's Mrs. Neeley. And what sort of I.D. do you need? Driver's license?"

"Yes. And passport. And birth certificate."

"Huh? You need to know if I was born in the USA?"

O'Conner grunted. "We will also need security clearance on every person who plans to work the DeVine wedding—from the local vendors, the ones we might have overlooked, to the servers. Can you provide us with a list so that we can contact them individually?"

"You really mean you're going to clear every single person working the wedding? Seriously?"

"Yes Ma'am. Every. Single. One."

"Ack." I led them to my office, where I attempted to piece together a list.

"Well, let's see. . .Hannah will be the photographer. At least, I think she will. Victoria hasn't specifically asked for her yet, but I usually use Hannah or her husband Drew to do the shoot."

"Do the shoot?"

"Right. Wedding shoot. Pictures." I held up my hands, as if holding an imaginary camera. "Click, click." A forced smile followed on my end, but he didn't play along. He just kept scribbling in that notepad of his.

"My friend Scarlet is doing the cake. You'll totally love Scarlet, by the way. She does great work. She's married to Armando, my brother. He's doing sound with D.J.."

"Armando Rossi? We've already run a check on him." O'Conner pursed his lips. "Doesn't have the cleanest record in the state."

"I know, I know. . .he has a bit of a history, but he's walking the straight and narrow now. He and Scarlet are expecting a baby. But that reminds me, Mama and Pop will be here."

"Cosmo Rossi." The agent nodded. "He checked out fine. So did your mother, Imelda. To be honest, Mrs. Neeley, you're the one we're concerned about."

"M-m-me?"

"Yes." He flipped through the pages of his notepad, finally landing on one that drew his undivided attention. "According to our research, you were arrested not once, but twice, over the past several years."

"Not true!" I put my hand up in the air, completely flustered by this accusation. "There was that one time—really, it was just a misunderstanding. Brock Benson thought he was protecting me from the paparazzi. How were we supposed to know they were police officers?" I gave him a scrutinizing look. "See now, if everyone dressed like you, it would be a lot easier to tell. But these officers weren't as believable. Anyway, the whole city rallied behind us and the charges were dropped. That's what happens when folks realize there's been a misunderstanding. They forgive and forget."

"We know all about it, Mrs. Neeley. Now, about your arrest in Splendora."

"Whoa, Nellie." I shook my head. "Let's set the record straight. I did *not* get arrested in Splendora. Just because I rode to the jailhouse in the back of the patrol car does not mean they locked me up. Again, the whole thing was a misunderstanding. I tried to explain to the officer that I hadn't stolen the almond extract from the Piggly Wiggly. It fell into my purse. He just took me in for questioning, that's all. He wanted to appease the store manager."

"Right." O'Conner gazed at the tablet. "No charges were filed. I see that now. I'm sure you can understand our concerns. Mr. DeVine is running for president of the United States. We need to make sure he's not surrounded by any suspicious characters."

"Suspicious characters, eh?" Uncle Laz popped his head into the office. "Did Bella tell you the story of how the Rossis have ties to the mob?"

I groaned and leaned my head down onto my desk. "It's. Not. True." I looked back up, my gaze shifting to Uncle Laz, who beamed like he'd just landed a role on a television sitcom. "My uncle Sal was in the mob, but he's dead now."

"They took him out?" Agent O'Conner scribbled in his notepad.

"No." I groaned. "He died of natural causes. And he wasn't technically my uncle."

"Sal Lucci was my brother from another mother." Uncle Laz squared his shoulders and puffed out his chest. "Never had a closer friend."

"And your best friend was in the mob?" The Secret Service guy stared with great intensity at my uncle. "Tell me more."

Laz took a few steps into the room and I could literally feel the Secret Service guys stiffening their backbones. "Well now, you see. . .once upon a time old Lazarro Rossi—yours truly—was a bit of a scoundrel. To say I was a heavy drinker would be putting it mildly. We lived in New Jersey at the time, and I was on my way home one night when suddenly, from out of nowhere, I had a Damascus Road experience."

"Damascus Road?" O'Conner looked up and I could read the confusion in his eyes. "Isn't Damascus in the Middle East?"

"Yep." Laz nodded and his eyes filled with tears, something that often happened when he shared his story. "See I was blinded by a bright light, just like the apostle Paul in the book of Acts."

I shook my head. "What he means to say is, he was stumbling out of a bar in a drunken stupor and landed in the middle of a street late at night. A city bus was headed right for him."

"As I said, a bright light." Laz squinted, as if seeing it all over again. "Back in those days, I was a vacuum cleaner salesman." He shifted his gaze to the Secret Service man. "For real, I mean. It wasn't a cover for anything else. Anyway, I sold a vacuum—a Kirby, model 516—to Sal, and the rest was history."

"He pulled you into the mob?" O'Conner asked.

"No. He pulled me into the bar. We were there together the night I saw the light. It took several years before he saw it too, but he did. Before he passed, praise the Lord."

"Sir, are you saying that your friend Sal Lucci was hit by a bus, as well? Is that how he died? If so, I would hardly call that natural causes."

"Oh, no. Not at all. Sal passed years later. He died with his hands and heart clean as a whistle, washed in the blood."

"Washed in blood?" O'Conner took to scribbling again. "Mob hit? His old life caught up with him?"

"No, his new life caught up with him. He died a happy man. And along the way, we even got Guido saved."

"You saved his friend?" O'Conner glanced up from his tablet. "From harm, you mean?"

"Yes, from harm. Saved Guido from a host of other issues, as well. He used to curse like a sailor."

"Mr. Lucci, you mean?"

"No, Guido." Laz grinned. "But we have a ways to go with Guido, if you want the truth of it. I doubt he'll ever make it all the way to the heaven, unless I tuck him under my arm when it's my time to go and we fly off to the great beyond together."

"You plan to take Guido to heaven?" O'Conner eyed Laz with more suspicion than before. "You've made that your mission?"

"That's the plan." Laz leaned back in his chair. "Kicking and screaming all the way, I dare say."

"Where is this Guido you speak of?"

"In the front hall."

Every man in the room startled to attention and they all began to argue over whether or not they'd passed a man named Guido in the front hallway of Club Wed.

"Calm down, everyone," I said. "Guido is just a parrot."

"In the figurative sense?" one of the men asked. "Meaning, he just repeats what he hears others say?"

"I knew a guy in the mob like that," O'Conner said. "Raised up from childhood with those thugs. Learned the lingo. Parroted everything they said. In his heart he didn't really mean it, though. He turned out to be a great guy."

"No," I debated. "He's a real, honest-to-goodness parrot. A bird. You passed him in the front hall."

"Oh, the bird." O'Conner scribbled something in his tablet. "Got it."

"That bird called me a heathen," one of the men said.

"And then sang *Amazing Grace*," another chimed in.

"After a couple of rounds of *100 Bottles of Beer on the Wall*," another added.

"You see my dilemma?" Laz sighed. "Poor old Guido can't make up his mind if he wants to go to heaven or...well, you know."

"So, let me get this straight." Agent O'Conner narrowed his gaze. "You weren't really in the mob, Mr. Rossi. And you, Mrs. Neeley, didn't do jail time. And Guido is really a bird, not someone you plan to take out."

"Right." Laz nodded. "Now you've got it. But this conversation is reminding me that I do need to let Guido out of his cage for a while. He needs to stretch his wings a bit."

"I see." O'Conner closed his tablet. "Please wait until after we're gone to release him. We'll get busy clearing the others in the family so that this event can move forward."

"Are you saying I should stop planning until you've cleared them?" I asked.

"Absolutely not. Please move forward with the plans. Mr. DeVine and Miss Brierley will be happy to know you're on task. The last thing we need right now is a distraction." He offered a strained smile and then shoved his notepad under his arm. "Now, just to fill you in, on the night of the wedding we'll have a Motorcade Support Unit here. They'll provide tactical support for official movements of motorcades."

"Wait. . .we're having motorcades?"

"Yes, but not until after the canine unit comes in for a sweep of the premises."

"Gosh, I'll have to get Guido out of here before then. He's not very good with dogs."

"Guido. The parrot."

"Yes. Guido, the parrot."

Laz started telling another story about Guido, but O'Conner cleared his throat. "Sir, we are the Secret Service. We don't have light conversation."

"You say that a lot." Laz patted O'Conner on the back. "You should have it tattooed on your arm."

"Mr. Rossi, I must inform you that Secret Service agents are prohibited from having visible body markings."

Laz's smile faded. "Oh, well I was just kidding about the tattoo."

"Not just tattoos, sir. We're not allowed to have body art or branding, and this would include any visible areas of the human anatomy, including but not limited to the head, the face, the neck the hands and the fingers."

"Oh, well I didn't really mean to imply that you—"

"If I were to get such a tattoo, I would be required to have it medically removed at my own expense in order to continue my duty to my country."

"I see. Well, I really was kidding about the tattoo." Laz shrugged.

"We don't kid, sir."

"I see that." Laz's gaze shifted to the door. I had a feeling he wanted to bolt.

"When one takes on the job of special agent, he—or she—takes the job very seriously. Very seriously." O'Conner lowered his glasses, squinted at Laz and then me with his blue eyes, and then put the glasses back in place. "I have a fulfilling career carrying out integrated missions of investigation and protection, folks. I work with others in my division to implement strategies to mitigate threats to some of our nation's finest leaders. No tattoo would be worth it. I'm sure you understand."

I understood all right. These guys didn't mess around. And they didn't have light conversation. And they were here to protect the future president of the United States, even if it meant driving the entire Rossi family to the brink of insanity in the process.

CHAPTER THREE
The Power of Love

The politicians were talking themselves red, white and blue in the face.
Clare Boothe Luce

On Thursday evening, January 14th, the family gathered at my parents' house to watch the Republican debate. Though we'd never been terribly political, knowing one of the participants first-hand suddenly gave us a vested interest.

We settled in in front of the television, bowls of popcorn in hand. Felt more like a movie theater experience than a political debate, but, with so many unknown variables, the popcorn felt right. So did the jokes from Uncle Laz, who insisted he'd rather be watching anything but a political debate.

"Lazarro Rossi, that's the trouble with you." Aunt Rosa slugged him on the arm. "You don't know what's going on in the world and you never will if you bury your head in the sand."

"I'm blissfully ignorant." He laughed. "There's nothing wrong with that. And we live on an island. There's plenty of sand to bury my head in, thank you very much. Don't mind if I do."

Rosa clucked her tongue. "But the world is in trouble and we need to be voting for someone who can make a difference."

Laz rolled his eyes. "Like any of them could make a difference."

"They can, if they trust God to use them," Mama said. "Hopefully a few of them will prove to be men—or women—of honor."

One by one the candidates were introduced. I recognized many of them, of course. So did Pop, apparently. He pointed out Donald Trump and started sputtering. "There he is. That's the guy who used to be on that show. What was it called, again? Celebrity something or another."

"Apprentice," D.J. said. "Celebrity Apprentice."

"Why couldn't things stay like they were? I always liked him on that show," Rosa said as she settled onto the loveseat next to Uncle Laz. "He was such a natural. He sat at his big desk and fired the ones who didn't get the job done. Remember how fun that was? Why did he have to spoil it all by running for president?"

"He's just one of many candidates," D.J. said.

"I see that," Pop said. "Looks like there are more Republican presidential candidates than there are Rossis." He slapped his knee and laughed. "And that's a lot of candidates!"

"Yep. Beau DeVine is just one of many," I explained. "From what I understand, he's pretty low in the polls right now but he made it onto the main stage for the debate, which is an honor. Not everyone makes it into the main debate."

"Which one is he, Bella?" Mama asked.

The camera panned the audience and I thought I caught a glimpse of Victoria. "Ooo, there's our bride!"

"She's running for president, too?" Pop asked. "I thought the only gal running for president was that Italian one."

"If you mean Carly Fiorina, I'm voting for her," Rosa said with a nod. "She's a good Italian girl and that goes a long way in my book."

"Actually, I'm pretty sure Fiorina is her married name," I said. "But I was talking about seeing the bride-to-be in the audience. And no, she's not running for President, Pop. She's engaged to—" My breath caught in my throat as Beau DeVine was introduced. "To him. To Beauregard."

"Carly Fiorina—the one who's not really Italian—is already married, but she's marrying a guy named Beauregard?" Pop took a handful of popcorn. "That's just weird. Don't they know that polygamy is illegal? What country are they from, anyway?"

"No, you're misunderstanding, Cosmo." Mama hit Pop with a pillow and the bowl of popcorn went flying across the room and landed on the floor, spilling everywhere. "Now look what you've done."

"What *I've* done?" He rolled his eyes. "These political candidates—the ones we're entrusting our country to—are leading secret lives and you're worried about a little popcorn on the rug?"

Mama knelt down and started picking up kernels and putting them in the bowl.

"They're not leading secret double-lives, Pop," I said.

"Well, I guess you're right. If this DeVine fellow is marrying a woman who's already got a husband and they're talking about it publicly I guess we could hardly call it a secret. But what's this world coming to, I ask you? We need folks we can trust in the White House, not people with loose morals."

"Well, the rest of you can vote for whoever you like." Mama looked up from her spot on the floor, her gaze resting on the TV screen. "I do believe I'm voting for that fellow right there, that young, handsome young man with the beautifully combed hair."

"Rubio?" D.J. shrugged. "He seems pretty solid."

"Oh, he's solid all right." Mama's eyes widened and she almost dropped the popcorn bowl. "Yes, I do believe I've found my candidate."

"We can't choose our candidates based on their heritage or their good looks," I reminded them. "We have to vote our conscience."

"My conscience says to vote for this guy." A funny smile turned up the edges of mama's lips. "But I promise to pray about it."

"Someone needs to pray," Pop said. "So many strange choices. Remember the old days, when it was easy to choose a candidate? You just voted for the person everyone else in the family voted for. These days everyone marches to their own drumbeat. Families divided. Not sure I like that."

"So, it makes more sense to vote for someone just because your uncle or son or brother tells you to?" Rosa rolled her eyes. "Those days are over. I want to make my own choices, even if it means no one else in the family speaks to me."

"I'll speak to you, honey." Laz pulled her close and planted a kiss on her forehead. "Even if you don't vote for me for president."

"You? You're running for president?" She snorted.

"Maybe."

"Well, if you decide to run, I'll definitely vote for you. Might be in the first time in years I truly believed in a candidate." Rosa give him a passionate kiss, right there in front of God and everybody.

"It'll be good to have your support." Laz said. "Makes a man feel like a winner to have a good woman behind him."

And that, I supposed, was what Beau DeVine was thinking right about now. Surely the love and support that Victoria offered gave him the courage to keep going, even when he didn't feel like it.

"So, where's that other lady?" Laz squinted at the TV. "The one we keep hearing so much about on the news."

"Hillary?" D.J. settled back on the sofa. "You won't be seeing her tonight. She's with the other party."

"She went to another party?" Laz yawned. "I can understand that. This one's a little boring, if you want my honest opinion. I'd go to another party, too, but no one invited me."

"Not a *party* party, Laz," Rosa said. "We're talking about a political party."

"I've seen those big political shindigs on the news and they don't look like much fun to me. All those people shaking hands and kissing babies and such. They'd be better off forgetting the parties and sticking to the things that matter."

"We're not saying Hillary is kissing babies, Laz. We're saying she's not debating tonight because she has different political ideologies. She's making a run for the White House too, but you won't see her during this evening's event."

"Ah. Gotcha." Uncle Laz calmed down.

Mama shook her head. "I just don't understand why Hillary would want to go back to the White House, anyway. I mean, if I ever made it out alive, I'd never go back."

"Maybe she wants to change the color of the drapes," Rosa suggested.

Mama shook her head. "The president doesn't change the drapes. There's got to be more to it than that."

"She could if she wanted," Rosa countered. "If she's the president."

"True." Mama nodded.

"Besides, I was speaking figuratively. Maybe she feels like her time there wasn't done, so she needs to go back to finish up."

"Maybe, but I still say, if I ever lived in the White House and made it out with my dignity intact, I would head home to Texas to live with the normals."

"Who are you calling normal?" Laz asked. "Speak for yourself."

"He has a point," D.J. added.

We settled down and watched the entire debate. Laz provided comic relief, and it would be an understatement to say that he didn't exactly care for Beau DeVine's answers. Still, we made it through the debate without anyone in the family getting too worked up. Well, except Mama. She appeared to swoon every time Marco Rubio came on the screen.

About ten minutes after the debate ended my cell phone rang. I was surprised when I saw Victoria's number on the other end. For some reason, visions of Secret Servicemen ran through my head. I answered to an exuberant squeal from the other end.

"Bella! Did you watch the debate?"

"I did. We all did."

"Thank you! Didn't my Beau-Beau do a great job?"

"Yes, he—"

"I mean, he really put a couple of those guys in their place, you know? And he showed those commentators a thing or two! He knows his stuff. And his numbers are up already. I think voters are responding to his answers."

"Sure. He did a great j—"

"Anyway, he had a great idea, and I love it, too. When I told him that your aunt and uncle have a show on the Food Network he asked if he could be a guest. See, Beau really loves to cook. He's great in the kitchen. And he wants people to see that side of him. He thinks he'll win over the female voters."

"Well, women aren't the only ones who cook, Victoria, so I'm not sure that's a—"

"Oh, I know. He just feels like the voters see him as this tough, firm candidate and that can be a little intimidating to female constituents. So, he wants to set the record straight and show them what a softie he is in the kitchen. And he's a great cook, too! You should taste his Veal Parmesan. It's so yummy. And we always laugh so much when we're cooking together. So, what do you say? Will you ask Rosa and Laz if they'll schedule an episode with Beau-Beau in it?"

"I could ask, but the Network always schedules their show in advance."

"We'll deal with the network. They'll be happy to have the future president on, I'm sure. So, if they're okay with it, do you think your aunt and uncle will be? I think they'll fall in love with my Beau-Beau."

I bit my tongue to keep from telling her that Uncle Laz had already formed an opinion of her sweet Beau-Beau. Before I could say, "I'll talk to them," she ended the call, her focus now on her husband-to-be.

"What was all that about, Bella?" D.J. asked. "Sounded strange."

"Um, yeah. Strange would be the right word." I turned my attention to my aunt. "She wants to know if you guys would have Beau as a guest on an upcoming episode. Turns out he makes a great Veal Parmesan."

Laz let out a grunt. "Let me guess. . .he wants to win over more voters?"

"I guess. But really, I think it might be fun. Don't you?" I offered what I hoped would look like a winning smile.

"Might be good for a few laughs," Laz said, and then quirked a brow. "At his expense, I mean."

"I'm afraid there wouldn't be much joking around," I countered. "The house will be filled with Secret Servicemen. You know?"

At this news, mama began to fan herself. "I don't know if I like this idea or not. I mean, it would be fun to one day say that we had the president of the

United States over to cook in our kitchen, but what if things don't go well? Then what?"

"Hey, it was his idea. And what could go wrong?"

D.J. gave me a "You've got to be kidding, right?" look but I did my best to ignore him. Well, until my father doubled over in laughter. Mama joined in and before long we were all talking about the comedic what-ifs. I had a feeling Beau and Victoria would be coming over to cook. . .and sooner, rather than later. How it would end? Well, that was anyone's guess.

CHAPTER FOUR
I Can't Help Falling in Love

Politics is too serious a matter to be left to the politicians.
Charles de Gaulle

Over the next couple of days Beau DeVine took a jump in the polls. Looked like several people really liked the guy. He'd won me over with a couple of his answers during the debate, but I still hadn't made up my mind yet.

Apparently Beau had some pull—not just in political circles, but with the Food Network, too. He managed to get himself scheduled for Rosa and Laz's next episode of The Italian Chef. Not that Beau was Italian. Or a chef, for that matter. Like Laz said, he probably just wanted to win over the voters. Still, the idea of having him in our home made my stomach churn, and not in a good way. I had to wonder why we couldn't spill the beans about the wedding venue when Beau was so willing to appear publicly on my aunt and uncle's show. I got my answer from Laz, who told me that the episode wouldn't air until Valentine's weekend. Even the Food Network had been sworn to secrecy. Go figure.

On the following Monday afternoon Beau and Victoria arrived at the Rossi home with a full entourage of Secret Servicemen. I wasn't sure who was more nervous—the bride-to-be or Mama and Pop, who'd never greeted a presidential candidate before.

The Secret Service fellas made an interesting complement to the Food Network crew, who seemed more than a little surprised to find themselves surrounded on every side by men in suits. Rosa took it all in stride, particularly once she got to know Beau in person. He personally pinned a "Go with Beau" button on her apron and she beamed with delight.

Laz, on the other hand, wouldn't take the button. "Sorry, dude." He put his hands up in the air. "Don't want to make a commitment just yet. Still haven't made up my mind. Lots of candidates to choose from. And I'm thinking of a run, myself."

"You are? Ah. I see." Beau looked a bit disappointed, as if he'd never been rejected before.

"Yep. After seeing the lineup the other night I thought I might just run for president, myself." Laz gave Beau a knowing look. "What do you think of them apples?"

"I think you're a little late to the party," Mama said. "Which clues me in to the fact that you're kidding."

"I'm not kidding at all." Laz crossed his arms at his chest. "I'm seriously thinking of running for President of the United States."

"Will you run as a Republican or Democrat?" Beau asked. "You'll need to decide quickly if you're going to get the party behind you."

"I will run as. . ." Laz paused and appeared to be thinking it through. "I'll create my own party. We'll call it the. . ." He pursed his lips. "I'll call it the Food Party. I'll be the first-ever Food Party candidate."

"Food Party?" Beau laughed and slapped his knee. "That's delicious. Get it? Delicious?"

Before long we were all laughing. Well, all but the Secret Service guys, who apparently didn't see the humor in Uncle Laz's joke.

"Yes, I'll be the best candidate anyone's ever seen," Laz added. "Feeding folks from coast to coast. That'll be my slogan. What do you think?"

"Feeding folks from coast to coast." Beau paused and appeared to be thinking seriously about my uncle's idea. "I think that's a noble cause, Lazarro. Kudos for thinking outside the box."

"That's me, an outside-the-box kind of guy." Laz slapped him on the back and Beau started coughing. This brought the Secret Service guys running. They backed away when Beau started laughing.

"Okay, let's get this show on the road. At least we're not making tea party foods tonight," Beau said. "We'll save that for the wedding."

"Interesting theme for a wedding." Laz said. "Never been to a tea party, myself."

"Right. I know it's different." Beau gave his bride-to-be a knowing look. "But, really, the whole tea party themed wedding was fine in my book. Kind of a political nod to the ultra-conservatives. They really seem to like me, and I want to keep that relationship strong."

"You're telling me that you themed your wedding to attract voters?" Mama looked flabbergasted by this notion. "Really?"

"Well, yes and no." The bride scooted into the spot next to Beau. "After all, my name *is* Victoria and I've always loved the Victorian era. So, it was a mutual decision, I assure you. The whole political slant is just a side note." She busied herself, putting on an apron on her husband-to-be, all chatter and nervous joking as she worked.

"Humph." Laz stepped into his position behind the island. "My candidacy is looking more reasonable every moment."

The conversation about politics shifted as the producer gave last minute instructions before filming. Minutes later, with the rest of us looking on from the hallway, the shoot got underway.

The episode started with Laz and Rosa cooking some of their Eggplant Parmesan. Yum. The tantalizing aromas wafting around the kitchen made me want to dive in. Alas, I could not. I had to keep my focus on their guest, the potential future president of the United States. Next, it was Beau's turn. He prepped the veal, chatting all the while.

"So, we're making Veal Parmesan, are we?" Uncle Laz asked. "One of my favorites."

"Mine too." Beau gave him a polite nod and kept working.

Turned out Beau DeVine was a consummate pro in front of the camera, even without a commentator feeding him questions. He knew just how to play to it with the correct angles and expressions. And I had to admit, he was shockingly handsome when one saw him up close. Dark hair, perfectly styled. Great skin. White teeth—suspiciously straight. Solid physique. Great suit. And he seemed to know his way around the kitchen, which won him over to Laz in a hurry. The guy had the perfect comeback to every joke, the ideal answer to every question, and the best possible camera angle for all of it.

Only one problem—he couldn't exactly focus on the skillet of veal while showing off. He tried to crack a joke, but somehow dropped a spatula into the hot oil, which splattered up and over the edge of the pan. The hot oil shot down into the fire below, and it began to blaze. Rosa let out a scream. A half-second later, the bottom of the skillet was in flames.

You would've thought the whole house was going up in smoke. The Secret Service stopped the shoot and a medic was called in to make sure Beau was okay. He was, of course. Rosa cleaned up the mess, salvaged the veal and the shoot got underway again in short order. Beau didn't look any worse for the wear, and neither did the veal, for that matter. Our guest of honor managed to get in a couple of political jokes.

"Oh, you like jokes, do you, Mr. DeVine?" Laz squared his shoulders. "Well, that's good, because I have a great one for you."

"Go for it, Lazarro." Beau continued his work on the veal, which, with the sauce and cheese, was starting to look very much like something Rosa and Laz would've concocted.

Uncle Laz reached over Beau to grab a wooden spoon. "Did you hear about the Italian chef who died?"

"No." Beau flipped the veal, revealing a golden crust.

"He pasta way." Laz slapped his leg. "Get it? *Pasta* way?"

Beau gave a polite chuckle, his gaze never leaving the skillet. "Good one, Lazarro. Good one."

"Now I have a question for you," Laz said. "Do you know what the word 'politics' means?"

"Well, of course." Beau looked squarely into the camera as he responded. "It—"

"It's from the word *poly*, which means *many*." Laz gave him a knowing look.

"Yes, of course, and—"

"And from the word *ticks* which means *blood sucking parasites*." Laz let out a raucous laugh and the cameraman started laughing so hard he almost dropped the camera. To my right, I saw Victoria flinch. O'Conner, who was standing to my left, didn't take the joke very well, either. He cleared his throat, a sure sign that we needed to get on with this before he interrupted the shoot again. Beau lifted the perfectly cooked veal from the skillet and placed in the empty platter in Rosa's hands.

"Didn't like that one, eh?" Laz's eyes narrowed. "Well, I have another one for you. What do you call a fake noodle?" Before Beau could respond, he hollered, "An *im*-pasta. Get it? An *im*-pasta? Ha-ha-ha-ha-ha!"

I had a feeling the Food network would be editing this episode. Heavily. For now, though, Rosa and Laz had to taste Beau's offering. He cut a couple of bite-sized pieces of the veal and I found my mouth watering. Rosa and Laz each grabbed a fork and dove in. Rosa's eyes closed and a delirious expression flooded over her face.

Laz's eyes widened as he swallowed. Afterwards, he gave Beau a slap on the back. "Young fella, I tell you what. . .that was some of the best Veal Parmesan I've ever eaten, and that's saying a lot."

"Why, thank you." Beau's cheeks flushed a deep crimson. "That means a lot coming from you, Mr. Rossi."

"Yes sir, some of the best I've eaten." Laz took his now-empty fork and pointed it at Beau's chest. "I'll make you a deal."

"Yes, sir?"

"If this whole running-for-President thing doesn't work out for you, you can always come and work at Parma Johns. We could use another good cook and I think you might be just the ticket."

"Well, I. . .I. . ." Beau cleared his throat and looked into the camera. "We all know that's not going to happen, but thank you kindly for the offer. You know what I always say. . .a well fed voter is a happy voter and a happy voter is happy to vote for DeVine."

"Hogwash." Laz took his fork and cut off another piece of veal and stuck it in his mouth. "Goofiest thing I've ever heard."

"Then perhaps you'll like my new motto," Beau added. "Feeding folks from coast to coast."

At this point, I thought Laz was going to slug him. He mumbled the words, "That jerk stole my slogan!" under his breath and his face turned beet-red.

Beau, probably trying to figure out a plan of escape, took a little nibble of the veal. A smile turned up the edges of his lips and the word "Delicioso!" followed.

Laz appeared to rally. He looked straight into the camera, his voice animated as he spoke: "I've seen a lot of cheese in this kitchen today, but not much of it has been on the food." He gave Beau a wallop on the back, which sent the poor fellow into a coughing fit. Just about the time he recovered, the director yelled cut and Victoria swept in to make sure her husband-to-be was okay. Rosa started scolding Laz, who went off on a tangent about blood-sucking politicians. Mama stood in the background looking mortified and Pop. . .well, he inched his way backwards out of the room.

I was tempted to do the same. Still, I knew I must stay and face the music—er, face the bride and groom. Likely there would be a bit of dust to settle after the lights and cameras were turned off.

CHAPTER FIVE

Love Takes Time

Do you ever get the feeling that the only reason we have elections is to find out if the polls were right?
Robert Orben

After the Food Network guys slipped out I caught a glimpse of the Secret Service fellows in the kitchen nibbling on leftovers. They seemed more relaxed than before, though one of them—a fellow with a mole on his cheek—kept a watchful eye on Beau, who followed Rosa and Laz out of the kitchen and into the living room. O'Conner dove into Uncle Laz's Eggplant Parmesan and a look of satisfaction came over him. He and the guys started talking about their favorite foods and before long everyone was relaxed and happy.

So much for 'No lighthearted conversation.'

Minutes later, we were all seated on the oversized sofas, relaxing. Mama and I served up cups of coffee and Laz kept Beau entertained with his Food Party campaign ideas. They started out okay, and our guests laughed at most, but after a while Laz got just plain silly.

"First, I think there should be a tax break for everyone who eats pizza at least once a week. Secondly, I believe—and I mean this with my whole heart—that we need to pass a law that families must eat together at the kitchen table at least three times a week. That's not asking too much. And, finally, I'm convinced we need to insist that families visit their homelands so that they never forget where they came from."

"Only, many of them don't really know where they came from," Mama countered. "You know? I have friends who are fourth or fifth-generation Texans. Maybe they don't know where their families originated."

"Then we should insist they go to one of those ancestry sites to find out." Laz nodded. "When I'm elected I'll propose a bill to Congress. Every man and woman should know his or her heritage. It's so important."

"What do you think, Beau?" my uncle asked after filling our ears with his ideas. "Will the voters go for that?"

At once, Beau's smile faded. The words, "I wish I knew what the voters wanted" threw us all for a loop. Just as quickly a forced smile lit his face. "I mean, I know what they want. They want someone fresh and new who will realign this country's moral compass. I plan to be that someone. And I think your ideas are terrific, Laz. Absolutely terrific." A fake smile followed.

In that moment, I saw a hint of pain in Victoria's eyes. Though she never said a word, I understood her. She was about to marry a fellow who had become one big sales pitch. Every word out of Beau's mouth was a slogan of some sort or a blurb about how he planned to save the country.

More than anything, I felt sorry for her. I could tell D.J. was uncomfortable with the dynamics between the two, as well. Instead of joining in the conversation, he offered to head over to Sophia and Tony's place to pick up our kids. Go figure.

I managed to hang on with political jargon eking its way out of Beau's mouth every few minutes. Laz didn't seem to mind. He just piggybacked on our guest's stories, offering his wacky solutions for the country.

Beau and Victoria left around seven o'clock. I arrived home in time to tuck the kids into bed. Afterwards D.J. and I settled in for the night.

"Was it just me, or did that guy seem a little. . ." My husband paused and shrugged.

"Fake?"

"I was going to say full of himself."

"Yeah. I guess all politicians come across that way, though. They talk about themselves and their plan to fix things. . .a lot, apparently." I paused and a memory came to me. "Hey, remember when Twila ran for mayor of Splendora last year? The other ladies couldn't stand being around her. She started believing her own press."

"Yes, but she finally repented. That's the difference, I guess. We know Twila. We trust her. With someone like Beau, you have to wonder if he can be trusted or if he's just canned air. You know?"

I shivered and then pulled the covers up to my chin. "Yeah but I'm getting to know Victoria and I think she's got a good head on her shoulders. She's a great gal who doesn't seem like the sort to make impulsive or foolish decisions, especially with something as big as her upcoming marriage. So, let's give her fiancé the benefit of the doubt, okay? And they're both Christians. . .or at least claim to be. So, maybe we're just not used to the whole 'campaigning' thing. You know?"

"Sounds like we'd better get used to it, if Laz is throwing his hat into the ring." D.J. snuggled up next to me and then laughed. "Can you even imagine your uncle in the White House?"

"Um, no." I got tickled, just thinking about it. "He'd be serving up pizza in the situation room."

"There would be quite a few 'situations' all right. And you know Rosa would redecorate the Oval Office. It would be Italian all the way." D.J. shuddered then leaned over and gave me a little kiss on the shoulder. "Every presidential painting would be surrounded by a gilded gold frame."

"I'd be more worried that Laz would keep Guido in there with him. He can't seem to part from that bird for more than a few hours at a time, but he doesn't do the best job keeping track of him. Remember that time Guido got loose and stole your dad's toupee?"

"Like I could ever forget that." D.J.'s kisses traveled up my shoulder to my neck and I giggled.

"Well, can you picture him flying around the White House, landing on some king or president's head?"

D.J. stopped kissing me and laughed. "Actually, I can. I can also picture him quoting scriptures to incoming heads of state."

"That might not be a bad thing."

"Until he belted out *100 Bottles of Beer on the Wall.* Then what?"

"Then Rosa would pacify her confused guests with some of her garlic twists and all would be well."

"True. Those garlic twists could certainly bring about world peace, don't you think?"

"Um, yeah. Or your mother's chicken fried steak. It's a close second."

"Mama. . .in the White House." D.J. laughed. "If Laz became President, no doubt my parents would show up for a visit."

"On their Harleys," I threw in. "With their *Bikers for Jesus* vests, of course."

"Of course."

"And the Splendora Sisters would show up wearing their glittery blouses with their bouffant hair and overly-made up faces."

"Wanting to sing at some big presidential event," D.J. added.

"And Laz would let them."

"And then the powers that be in D.C. would fall in love with them and they'd be asked to perform regularly, which would mean Twila would have to give up her job as mayor of Splendora. And before long heads of state would be seeking the ladies out for their opinions on political matters."

"They would give their opinions," I added. "Probably on TV. Maybe the Larry King show."

"Larry King's retired."

"Right." I paused to think it through. "Jimmy Fallon. He'd do some sort of spoof with them. It would be hilarious. But the country would fall in love with them and before long they'd be asked to run for Congress. Or, better yet, Laz would appoint them to the Supreme Court."

"Things would really get interesting then." D.J.'s eyes widened. "Can you even imagine Twila, Bonnie Sue and Jolene sitting on the bench?"

"I can't imagine them sitting still that long. . .anywhere. And they certainly wouldn't agree to wear the robes. Not without glittery collars, anyway."

"Right?" D.J. grinned.

"I don't know why we're talking about this, anyway. It's not like Uncle Laz is really going to run for President, anyway. He doesn't even know where he stands on the issues. If you ask him about global warming he tells you that he gave up electric blankets when we moved to the south." For whatever reason, this got me tickled. I laughed until I lost my breath.

D.J. laughed, too, and leaned back against his pillows as he calmed down. "To be honest, I'm not sure Beau knows where he stands. . .on anything. Do you get the idea that he's a little unsure of himself? When the cameras are turned off, I mean."

"Definitely."

D.J. sighed. "I hope—and I don't really know the guy—but I hope he's not just going through with this to try to prove something to himself or anyone else. Sometimes people get into things and feel like they can't get out. Take the year I signed up for t-ball because my dad thought I should. I joined the team and there was no way out of it. Toughest year of my young life."

"I thought you loved playing ball."

"Nah, that was my brother. I was never very good at it. But I didn't want to hurt my dad's feelings. He wanted it for me, so I gave it my best shot. Maybe that's what Beau's doing too."

"Maybe. Not sure who he's trying to impress, though. I can tell you one thing, it's not Victoria. I suspect she'd be just as happy if he went back to work at the law firm he started a few years back."

"Can't blame her there." D.J. yawned. "Can you imagine how different life would be in the White House? I'm trying to imagine us living there with the kids."

"Um, no." I cringed. "For one thing, how would we keep those four rowdies from tearing everything up? I'd look away for a second and some priceless keepsake signed by Abraham Lincoln would be turned into a paper airplane by Tres. Or some heirloom purchased by Mamie Eisenhower would be shattered by Rosie. And the twins would insist on being held during every Cabinet meeting. You know?"

"I'd be more worried that you and I would never have any alone time." D.J. gave me a funny look. "Do you think the presidential quarters have video cameras?"

"Ack. Never thought about it." My imagination kicked into overdrive and I felt my cheeks grow warm.

D.J. leaned over and kissed my cheek. "A fella needs his privacy when he's got a gal as pretty as you."

"O-oh?" I giggled as he kissed my ear. "Why is that?"

"Because, Bella Neeley, I couldn't very well do this with the cameras rolling." His kisses traveled down my neck to my shoulder.

Delicious shivers came over me as I enjoyed his nearness. "Mmm. I see." A contented sigh followed on my end. "No, you couldn't."

"Guess I'll never be president, then." His gentle kisses moved down my arm and my eyes fluttered close. "Hope you don't mind."

"Mind? Um, no, I don't mind. You don't have to be anything. . .but you."

As his lips traveled back up my arm and eventually met mine for a kiss that set off fireworks, I had to conclude the obvious: D.J. Neeley might not be Oval Office material—he might not save the country from ruin—but he was all this little gal from Texas would ever need.

CHAPTER SIX
Crazy Little Thing Called Love

There might be some serious fun in politics.
Hunter S. Thompson

In spite of my heavy workload, I did my best to focus on my family over the next several days. It felt so good to be home again, with our babies. We'd both missed them terribly while on our cruise. And it looked like they'd missed us, too. I could hardly get the twins to leave my side for more than a minute without crying. And Tres, from what we'd been told by his teacher, was struggling through first grade. Little Rosie—the apple of her Aunt Rosa's eye—was a typical preschooler, filled with rambunctious shenanigans. And though these four kiddos kept us on our toes, D.J. and I loved, loved, loved being with them. We'd enjoyed our time away, of course. And though we'd had a wonderful time—Santorini being high on my list of places we'd visited—there was something to be said for the phrase, "There's no place like home."

Home, of course, meant family.

And family, of course, meant chaos.

And that's what we'd come to expect every time the Rossi and Neeley families came together. We anticipated nothing less when D.J.'s parents invited the whole Rossi clan to hang out with them in Splendora on Saturday, the 23rd of January. I could hardly wait to see my in-laws—and the rest of our Splendora friends, too. I particularly loved the idea of meeting at Bubba's BBQ, the restaurant my best friend and her husband owned. I couldn't remember the last time I'd seen Jenna and Bubba. We were long overdue for a visit.

Though the weather was cold and wet, the family atmosphere was warm and cozy. Gathered around sturdy picnic tables inside of Bubba and Jenna's family-style restaurant, we chowed down on ribs, smoked turkey, brisket and sausage links. I loved every bite, but what really made my day was the people who gathered around us. Jenna. Bubba. Earline. Dwayne, Sr. Twila, Bonnie Sue, Jolene. . .and all of their respective spouses.

Jenna and I gabbed like we'd been apart for years, and all the more when two of our friends—Lily and Jasmine—joined us. At this point the BBQ joint came alive with voices overlapping and people hugging. The kids had the time of their lives, hanging out with old friends and getting smooches from their Splendora grandparents.

Everything was perfect. . .until Uncle Laz brought up politics. I knew from my years of experience that one never brought up politics around my mother-in-law unless one planned to get an earful. Anyone with any common sense at all didn't go there. Ever.

Unfortunately, Laz hadn't gotten the "Don't mess with Earline" memo. About halfway into our dessert he announced to the group that he was planning to run for president of the United States representing the brand-spanking new Food Party.

Earline's eyes narrowed to slits. "Lazarro, am I to understand you're *seriously* runnin' for office?"

"Sure. I'm having yard signs made and everything. And buttons, too. That whole thing'll be a hoot. Do I have your support, Earline? I need a campaign manager, if you're interested in the position. I pay in pizza and pasta." He gave her a playful wink and then took another bite of his banana pudding.

She grew silent and I had a feeling her next words would not be encouraging. After a moment she released a slow breath, followed by the words, "So, the electoral process is nothing but a big joke to you? Is that it? You don't see the gravity of the situation? This is a just a game to you?"

"Uh-oh." Jenna rose and headed toward the kitchen.

D.J. made an exaggerated clucking noise as she disappeared from view. Not that I blamed her. I was a chicken, too. In fact, I would've run, myself, if I didn't have four small children to tend to.

Uncle Laz looked genuinely hurt by Earline's notion. "Of course it's not a game to me. I just, well. . ."

"Earline, honey. . ." D.J.'s dad put his hand on her knee. "Now, Laz's just havin' a little fun to ease the tension. It's been a tough political season. A good laugh never hurt anyone, especially now."

"I beg to differ," she countered. "Our country is in serious trouble. There's no time for fun. This is a critical season we're in, one that calls for prayer and intercession, not joking around."

I tugged at my collar. Was it suddenly getting hot in here?

"Well, yes," D.J. added. "But someone needs to break the tension. A little comic relief is good, as Pop said. There's no point in folks getting in a knot over things." He took another bite of brisket and a satisfied look came over him. "This meat is really good."

"One thing I cannot abide, truly, is people who don't see the seriousness of where we're headed as a nation." Earline began to fan herself. "Either you care about this country's well-being or you don't. Either you vote to change the course of a nation or you don't."

Mama looked a bit perplexed by this. "Now, Earline, don't throw the baby out with the bath-water. We all care about our country, but we don't all vote the same."

At this point Earline rose and began to pace the room. "Oh, but we must. We must be like-minded. We've got to agree or let our disagreements topple the whole thing. At this point we cannot—and I repeat, cannot—afford to let the whole thing topple. There's too much at stake."

"I plan to vote my conscience," Rosa said. "And trying to get the rest of the group to go along with me is impossible, even on the best of days. I can't even get them to agree on what I should make for dinner, let alone who should be president."

"Which is exactly why we must research. Diligence is key." Earline shuddered. "My goodness, is it hot in here or what? Has someone adjusted the thermostat?"

It was hot, all right, but it didn't have as much to do with the temperature as one might imagine.

Jenna returned with extra bowls of banana pudding. "Here you go, folks. The perfect way to make everyone happy again. Let's all settle in and have a good time. No more squabbling about politics. It'll be Valentine's Day soon—a time to remember why we love each other."

I was pretty sure they didn't hear a word she said. The bickering continued between Laz and Earline, who sat back down and took a couple of bites of banana pudding. Before long, Twila got involved. Turned out her views were just as strong as Earline's, though they disagreed on which candidate was right for the job. Then Jolene made the mistake of saying she might switch to a different political party. This really set things off. She and Rosa took sides against Earline and Twila, who got pretty vocal. Laz carried on about the Food Party and managed to convince Bonnie Sue that she should serve as his campaign manager. Mama continued to fan herself and Pop ate all of the leftover banana pudding, since no one else was looking.

D.J. sat to my left, nibbling on pork ribs. When Tres said, "Daddy, why are they fighting?" my sweet husband just shook his head and said, "Ask your mother."

"Mommy?" Tres looked at me and I sighed.

"They're just having a discussion, honey. They really love each other."

"They do?" Tres called out as the noise level rose. "Really?"

"Yes." I raised my voice to be heard above the din. "We do love each other, don't we, Rossis and Neeleys? My son is beginning to wonder!"

"Well, a'course we love one another." Earline dismissed the idea with a wave of a hand, then went back to arguing with Rosa and Laz. Before long, Dwayne Sr. joined in. Jenna leaned our way and put her finger over her lips.

"Um, folks. . .?"

No one responded.

"Hey, everyone. . ." she tried again.

Still, no one responded.

"For the love of all that's holy," she screamed. "Quiet down in here! We have other customers and they're complaining about the noise! This is a family restaurant. You know?"

I knew, all right. Poor Jenna. And poor Bubba! He stuck his head out of the kitchen door and hollered, "Do I need to call 9-1-1?"

"No. Just please ask your family to keep it down." Jenna mumbled something under her breath and headed across the restaurant to wait on other customers.

I sighed as I shifted my gaze back to Earline and Laz, who were having it out over whether the U.S. should—or shouldn't—provide shelter for refugees from war-torn countries. That discussion sent the participants over the edge. Laz turned red in the face. Earline turned redder. On and on they went, until I felt sure the police would be called in to break up the fight.

Fortunately, it all came to a quick end. Twila decided to stop mid-squabble and pray. Aloud. For all to hear. She pleaded God's mercy on our family, Laz's politics, and on our nation as a whole. If that didn't make the folks at the next table feel better, nothing would.

They got up and left mid-prayer. I only knew this because my eyes were wide open so that I could keep an eye on my kids, who were chiming in with an occasional "Amen!"

When the prayer ended, everyone simmered down. Well, all but Mama, who looked so flustered she couldn't seem to string two words together. Pop asked Dwayne Sr. to pass an untouched bowl of banana pudding and before long we were all eating in silence.

Awkward silence.

Still, awkward silence was better than awkward fighting, so I would take it.

By the time Jenna arrived with the coffee pot, Earline seemed to be in better spirits. Either the Lord had calmed her heart or she'd forgotten to be mad at Uncle Laz. Likely, the first.

Things went really well until it came time to pay the bill. Pop offered to pick up the tab, which got Dwayne and Earline flustered. Somehow, this led back around to a discussion about money, which led—once again—to politics. At this point Laz announced to the family two tables over that he was running for president. They pulled out their cell phones and started taking pictures of him. A couple of them uploaded the photos to social media.

Great. Now this whole thing would probably go viral and Uncle Laz really would have to run for president.

"At least I've got some good ideas," Laz said. "Better than that guy with all the slogans, the one who's getting married at Club—" Laz put his hand over his mouth and his eyes widened. "Sorry, Bella."

"Wait." Bonnie Sue's gaze narrowed and she looked my way. "There's something you're not telling us, Bella. Who's getting married at Club Wed? Someone political?"

"Yes, who is it, Bella?" Lily asked me. "Someone we would know?"

Ack. So much for keeping things on the down-low.

"She's not allowed to say." Mama fanned herself. "But it's someone important. Very important."

"Top secret." Pop took a swig of his coffee. "If we tell you, we'll have to kill you."

"Oh my." Bonnie Sue paled. "Then please don't tell me. I have a few good years left, after all."

"I'd like to stay alive, as well," Jolene said. "Guess you'll have to fill us in after-the-fact, Bella. Okay?"

"Okay. I promise I'll tell you when it's over. For now, though, we've been asked not to say anything publicly, so please don't ask."

"Ooo, I'll bet I can guess." Earline grinned. "That handsome Brock Benson is coming back, isn't he?"

"Nope. Not Brock. Please don't ask me any more questions, okay?"

"Okay." Earline gave me a suspicious look. "But I'll be waiting on pins and needles."

She wasn't the only one. I glanced around the BBQ joint just to make sure Agent O'Conner wasn't seated nearby with any of his men. Nope, no one in a suit. A fella would stick out like a sore thumb, wearing a suit in the town of Splendora. Still, the idea that we might've just given away top secret information left me feeling a little squeamish inside.

Or maybe it was the combination of too much banana pudding and politics. Hopefully those two wouldn't turn out to be a deadly combination.

CHAPTER SEVEN
Unchained Melody

We hang the petty thieves and appoint the great ones to public office.
Aesop

We somehow survived the political brou-ha-ha and forged ahead into the next week. I'd almost forgotten about the craziness of our family get-together until I received a call from Victoria the next Thursday. She sounded more wound up than ever, and I had a feeling it would take some serious wedding coordinator skills on my part to calm her down.

"I don't mind admitting I'm getting nervous, Bella." Her words came out shaky and faint.

"Why?" I shifted the phone to my other ear to better hear her. She must be out on the road again, traveling with Beau. Maybe they were driving through a tunnel or something.

"It's the 28th of January. My wedding is in a little more than two weeks and I'm not feeling the Valentine's spirit yet."

"Well, no one is. Except the stores, I mean. They're loaded with candy and decorations, but other than that—"

"I'm so caught up in the rush-rush-rush of getting from one campaign event to another, from one debate to another, that I'm barely able to think clearly about the wedding."

"That's why you've hired me, honey. I've implemented dozens of ideas since we spoke last. Do you have a minute to listen to them? Or, would it be better if we Skyped so I could show you the pictures I've collected?"

"Can't Skype right now. I'm getting dressed for the debate. Sorry."

"No need to apologize." And that explained where she was at the moment. "I'd almost forgotten about tonight's debate. I guess we won't be watching this time. D.J. and I have Bible study and the rest of the family is going to the movies."

"That's okay. I understand. But don't you see my point? You guys are living a normal life, not caught up in the political stuff. I'm about to be a bride, for pity's sake. I should be stressed about my wedding, not an election, right? I mean, what kind of bride is so caught up in a presidential race that she doesn't have time to discuss her wedding?"

"We're discussing it now. And please don't fret. You've got two weeks. So, deep breath."

"This just isn't like me. I'm the organized one. Very OCD. From the time I was a little girl I had all my ducks in a row. So the idea that I'm off in—where are we again? Oh, right, Iowa—means that I've become someone other than who I used to be."

"You're in love with a man who's running for the highest office in the land. Don't be so hard on yourself."

She sighed. "That's another part of me you don't know. I'm always hardest on myself. I find it rather remarkable that I haven't had a major breakdown by now."

"Well, hold off on the breakdown till after the wedding, okay? And just leave everything to me. Want me to fill you in on the things I've already done?"

"Please."

"Okay. Let's start with the food. I spoke to the caterer and we've finalized the menu. It's going to be amazing. As far as desserts go, Scarlet has promised her most beautiful cake yet. She also had the best idea for teacup shaped cookies. And teapots, too. We can wrap them individually and put them at each place setting as a gift. What do you think?"

"Sounds great."

"She can even monogram them with your initials. It'll be classy looking. Scarlet wanted me to pass along some sketches of the cake. I think you're going to love it. It's Victorian, through and through, and in your color scheme."

"How horrible is it that I haven't even had time to talk to my own cake decorator, Bella?" Victoria released a groan. "What kind of bride lets her coordinator do everything?"

"The kind who's trying to help her fiancé win a bid at the White House."

"Hmm." She paused and I read doubt in the blank space.

"Anyway, I think you're going to love the table settings. I have a vendor in Houston that specializes in fine china. They've found a pattern that's perfect. I'll send you a picture, if you like, but trust me. . .it matches the cake, the flowers, everything. It's divine."

At this, she laughed. "I get it. DeVine."

"Oh, right." I chuckled. "Anyway, it's the most beautiful Victorian pattern you've ever seen. Perfect for Valentine's and ideal for a tea party."

"Tea party." She sighed. "You do think the tea party idea is going to be pretty, right? I mean, I'm not just going along with it because of Beau—though he does love the idea. I hope my guests don't think it's too. . .political. You know? Do you think my guests will read too much into this?"

"No, not at all. They'll just think it's lovely."

"Yeah. I hope so. Not that my guests even know where the wedding is going to be held. Craziest wedding invitations ever. Guests were all instructed to wait for a phone call the day ahead. My poor aunt from Montana didn't even know how to go about booking her flight until I told her it was close to Houston. That's all they would let us say to our guests. And don't even get me started on the chaos this has caused between my parents and Beau's mother. Everyone's up in arms."

"It's just a season, Victoria. You know? I've been through seasons that I thought were impossible, but they all came to an end and a new season started. You'll see."

"If he wins the election, though. . ." Her words drifted off and an uncomfortable silence rose up between us. "I hate to even say those words because he's so determined, so convinced he's going to be the next president of the United States." Another pause followed. "Which would make me the first lady. And what kind of first lady would I be if I don't even take the time to design my own wedding cake? How can I take on the problems of the country if I let someone else pick out the china for my wedding reception?"

"You'd be like every other first lady in the history of first ladies. Do you really think they have the time to deal with the finer details? Of course not. They have people for that. Just relax, Victoria, and let me be your people. It's what I do. It's what I love to do."

"You don't mind?" She sniffled.

"Not at all."

I somehow managed to get her calmed down, and before long we were enmeshed in a conversation about the upcoming ceremony. I promised to send her pictures of china patterns, along with the sketches Scarlet had sent over. Then we turned our attention to the flowers.

"My good friend Cassia runs the flower shop here," I explained. "She's the best. I've told her to order two thousand flowers in various shades of pink, lavender and ivory. She was beside herself. I've never seen her this excited." A pause followed. "You know, I really have to thank you, Victoria. My vendors have never done a ceremony this big before. Your wedding is bringing some much-needed income to the island. So, instead of apologizing, you need to know how grateful we are. When all is said and done, we'll have the honor of saying we hosted the wedding of the century for the man and woman who could potentially be the president and first lady of the United States."

"Right." She paused. "Potentially."

Just one little word. But I had a feeling that word was the driving force in Victoria Felicity Brierley's life right now.

"If I could just see into the future, I think I'd be a lot calmer." She sighed. "You know?"

"I know there have been a lot of times in my life when I wished I knew what was coming. But, in retrospect, I'm kind of glad I didn't know. I mean, what if things don't turn out the way you want? What if he doesn't win? Won't you be glad you didn't see that coming?"

There. I'd said the words aloud.

"Beau-Beau would be devastated." Victoria's voice grew faint again.

"And you?"

"I. . .I. . ." She paused and then said, "Sorry, Bella. Have to go. They're telling me it's almost time. Wish him luck, okay?"

"I'll pray for him, Victoria. Praying for God's best."

"Thanks, Bella. We appreciate it."

I knew she meant those last words, and I also knew that praying for God's best might result in a different outcome than she hoped for.

Then again, from the tone of her voice, maybe Victoria Felicity Brierley wasn't really sure what to hope for. One had to wonder, anyway.

CHAPTER EIGHT
I Can't Stop Loving You

When I was a boy I was told that anybody could become President; I'm beginning to believe it.
Clarence Darrow

On the morning of February 1st Uncle Laz placed a large sign in the front yard of the Rossi home that read *Lazarro Rossi for President*. According to my brother Nick he also hung two large posters in Parma Johns with similar wording, which had created quite a buzz among the customers. I couldn't help but wonder what prompted my uncle to make a spectacle of our family like this, but what could I do to stop him? And I shuddered every time I thought about how Earline would react, once she found out. No doubt she would take him to task. Or question his sanity. The rest of us were already doing that.

I gave the sign in the yard a closer look as I pulled into the driveway of Club Wed next door. Looked like he'd used a pizza box to make it. Not the most professional approach, but it did seem to go along with his "Food Party" theme.

Theme.

Just thinking of the word reminded me of the upcoming tea party wedding. I needed to place a call to the caterers. After speaking with them I remembered that I needed to check in with my other vendors. I decided to set up a group call that included Scarlet, Gabi, Cassia and Hannah—the cake decorator, wedding dress designer, florist and photographer. Ten minutes later, I had everyone on the line. Hearing all of them at once wasn't a piece of cake. They gabbed like BFFs who hadn't seen each other for months. Should I remind them that they all lived within three miles of each other? Nah. I'd let them have a good time and then shift gears to talk about the wedding.

"Ladies, are you ready?" I asked when my patience wore thin.

"Ready," Hannah said.

"Me too," Scarlet chimed in.

"I'm here, Bella," Gabi added.

"And me," Cassia interjected. "Can't wait!"

"Okay, before we talk about anything else, I wanted to let you know that we've hired a caterer this time around. It just made sense. Just got off the phone with them. We've finalized the list of appetizers and foods."

"Why?" Hannah sounded genuinely perplexed.

"Because I don't really know much about the kinds of foods Beau wants and, to be honest, I'm terrified of someone getting food poisoning or something random like that."

Scarlet laughed. "Bella, please. With all of the weddings you guys have done, has anyone ever gotten food poisoning?"

"No, but this would be the time it would happen. And trust me when I say we're perplexed about the menu. It's over our heads. Fancy stuff. You know?"

"Like what?" she asked.

"Ham, Brie and Apple Spread , Crab Louie Salad with Horseradish Panna Cotta, Spicy Tuna Tartare in a Sesame Miso Cone, Chinois Chicken salad in Miniature Won Ton Shells. . .and a ton of other things I can't pronounce, most of it finger-food sized to fit the garden party theme. Earl Grey Pots de Creme, smoked trout with sliced cucumber and onion. And then there are the sweets: Orange-Cardamom Madeleines, petit fours in five different colors to match the plates, Almond scones with lemon curd and fresh raspberries. . .shall I go on?"

"Wow. I've never even tasted half of that stuff," Scarlet said. "And I work in a kitchen."

"Right?" I said. "Neither have any of us. So, how would we know if it came out right? We wouldn't. Rosa doesn't trust herself to do it and Laz just laughed when I gave him the list."

"That says a lot," Hannah chimed in. "Those two can cook just about anything."

"Yep. We're being cautious, though. We want the very best for these folks, so I've hired a high-end caterer from the River Oaks area in Houston. One of my brides used them a couple of years back. They're very professional, and best of all, the groom actually knows the owner and loves the idea. They're both happy. And we're happy *not* to be responsible for it."

"Well, that's happy news." Cassia laughed. "My family's in the restaurant business and I don't have a clue about any of those things you just listed. Is that what politicians eat?"

"Who knows what politicians eat. I just know that Rosa and Laz don't want to cook. And it's a huge relief not to have to fill the table ourselves. Did I happen to mention that we didn't know the groom-to-be was running for president of the United States when these two put down their deposit to use Club Wed?"

"No way!" Hannah laughed. "Are you saying that you just found out when we did?"

"Pretty much. I got the first call from Victoria back in December when I was working on Justine's wedding and she never mentioned his presidential run. I just found out when we got back from our cruise. So, um, yeah. . .I was a little stunned."

"Wait, Justine?" Hannah echoed. "You did a wedding for a Justine? Did I do the photos?"

"The meteorologist," Scarlet threw in. "The one with the Christmas wedding."

"Oh yeah. I remember now." Hannah laughed. "They're all running together in my brain."

"Mine too." Gabi sighed. "I've been eating, sleeping and breathing wedding gowns."

"I remember Justine," Cassia said. "She thought she was going to have the ceremony outdoors but a freak snowstorm changed everything."

"That's the one. So, we go from having a freak snowstorm in December to the president—er, potential president—getting married at Club Wed on Valentine's Day. Kind of makes me wonder what's coming next." A shiver ran down my spine all of a sudden. I did my best to shake it off.

"Well, I guess you could say that God is opening doors for you, Bella," Scarlet said. "You prayed for that, you know. Long before you and D.J. opened the facility in Splendora, if memory serves me correctly. Way back in the early days, when you first took over Club Wed you prayed that God would bring in clients."

"True."

"And now He's doing it."

"True again." I laughed. "If you had told me years ago that I would be hosting weddings for Hollywood stars and presidential candidates I would've said you were crazy."

"And yet, here you are." She gave me a knowing look.

"Did you gals get 'the visit' from the Secret Service guys?" Cassia asked. "Scared me to death, and you don't even want to know what my parents thought when they showed up at *Super Gyros* right as Mama was closing up."

"Now you've piqued my curiosity." Scarlet laughed. "What did your parents think?"

"Babbas thought for sure it was the health inspector, come to shut down the family restaurant. Scared him to death. I think it was all the suits."

"Drew thought they were from the IRS," Hannah said. "In fact, he still thinks that."

"Armando knew who they were," Scarlet said. "But it still freaked him out. He's not used to being watched that closely. They are a little creepy, don't you think?"

"Creepy's the right word." I shivered. "But I'm sure they're just regular guys. Take those dark suits away and you've got—"

"Some really buff guys in their boxers," Scarlet said and then laughed. "Okay, okay, don't tell Armando I said that, but those guys are really. . ."

"Solid?" Hannah said.

"To say the least. I guess I'll never work for the Secret Service. I'm too fluffy."

"And you're having a baby, Scarlet. I'm pretty sure they won't be hiring you any time soon."

"True. Not that I envy them, anyway. I wouldn't want to be away from my family like that. You know?"

Silence rose up between us. Hannah interrupted it with a question. "Did that strike a chord, Bella?"

"Sort of." I sighed. "It's okay. I'm just tired. Trying to balance life with four kids, a husband, a big family and crazy weddings. . .well, it's starting to wear on me."

"I understand. Drew and I only have one child and we're tired all the time."

"Can you imagine being in Victoria's place?" Cassia asked. "I mean she and Beau are on the road every day, and they always have to put on their happy face, to be publicity ready. I can't put on my happy face when I'm really down in the dumps, so I don't know how they do it."

"Yeah, I've wondered the same thing. And I have to wonder—this is just me, speculating—I have to wonder if they're both as happy and positive as they let on. They remind me of a couple of professional ball players on a team that's headed to the playoffs. The hype is there. The drive is there. But so is the fear that they won't really win the game, after all."

"Are you saying that she's worried he'll lose?" Scarlet asked.

"At this point, she might be more worried that he'll win. But that's just speculation on my part. Please don't quote me on that." I flinched as I realized

I'd just spoken my thoughts aloud to my friends. I also found myself wondering if my phone was bugged. Oh well. The Secret Service guys were probably wondering the same thing.

"Is it true that your Uncle Laz is running for President?" Hannah asked. "He asked if he could put a poster in our studio window."

"I saw it at Parma John's," Scarlet said. "Crazy, that he's going through with this."

"Babbas let him put up a poster at Super Gyros too," Cassia added. "I guess it's true, then?"

"He's going to take this joke as far as people will let him," I said. "So folks have got to stop encouraging him."

"Are you kidding? Everyone on the island is all over the idea." Hannah laughed. "Laz talked the mayor into being his campaign manager."

"Bonnie Sue will be devastated," I explained. "He talked her into the very same thing."

"I guess they can duke it out." Scarlet said. "Can you imagine Bonnie Sue and the mayor in a fist-fight?"

This led the ladies to a completely different conversation. On and on they went, talking about what life would be like with my uncle as president of the United States, Bonnie Sue and the mayor guiding him every step of the way. Before long, they'd drawn me in. All of my anxieties lifted as our giggles turned to chuckles and our chuckles to full-blown laughter.

In that moment, a realization hit. With these gals at my side, I could handle just about anything life threw my way. . .even a wacky uncle and an upcoming wedding with Secret Service agents as the guests of honor.

CHAPTER NINE

I Want to Know What Love Is

Politics, it seems to me, for years, or all too long, has been concerned with right or left instead of right or wrong.
Richard Armour

I didn't claim to know much about politics but I did understand how the primaries worked. Mostly. On the 9th of February, just a few days shy of the wedding of the century, voters lined up at the polls in a faraway state called New Hampshire. There they would give some indication of Beau DeVine's standings in the presidential race. If the news stations could be believed, big decisions would be made, based on the outcome.

Not that I had time to think about the presidential race. I had other things on my mind: finalizing details for Beau and Victoria's wedding. And even though this was just Tuesday, I felt as if things were now moving in warp speed. Half of me was terrified; the other half was happy to know the whole thing would soon be behind us.

I headed up to Parma Johns at lunchtime to meet with Scarlet. I needed to let her know that the guest list had grown by forty. This was now officially our largest wedding ever. Where we would put all of the guests, I had no idea. We'd have to squeeze them into Club Wed like sardines.

Speaking of squeezing people in, I found Parma Johns crowded with lunch customers. Dean Martin's *Pennies From Heaven* played over the loudspeaker and people munched down on the shop's daily special, a large meatball pizza. Yum. I'd like to have a bite of that, myself. But first, to find Scarlet. I headed through the crowd to her adjoining bakery, *Let Them Eat Cake.*

Before I could make it, though, Galveston's mayor rushed my way. He put his hand on my shoulder. "Bella, did you hear?"

"Hear what?"

"A reporter from the *New York Times* is in town asking lots of questions. Why didn't you tell me that we had a presidential candidate coming to town? I would've put up banners or something. This is a very big deal."

"Wait. . .what?"

"Beau DeVine is getting married at Club Wed? Sunday night? This would've been helpful information."

"But Mayor Bradley, it's supposed to be top secret information. No one is allowed to know except the vendors and they're sworn to secrecy."

"Well, the cat's out of the bag now. See that fella right over there?" The mayor pointed to a table where a man with salt and pepper hair sat across from Mrs. Hightower, one of the island's most well-to-do women. "That's a Mr. Jamison from New York City. Yep, New York City, sitting right here in Parma Johns on Galveston Island. He works for the *New York Times*. We're going to be famous, thanks to this wedding." He straightened his tie. "Do I look alright? I don't have pizza sauce on my face, do I?"

"You look fine. But why is he talking to Mrs. Hightower?" I asked.

"Because she's the head of the Republican Women's League here in Galveston, so he thinks he can get some information out of her. This is all so exciting. I mean, your little wedding facility is really putting Galveston on the map. But you owe us all an apology for not cluing us in sooner. Shame on you."

I wasn't sure which irritated me more—the fact that the mayor of Galveston had just called Club Wed a 'little' facility, or the idea that he thought I was just now putting Galveston on the map. Hadn't we already done that when Brock Benson—star of stage and screen—came to town? And what was up with this reporter dude sailing into town and blowing our cover? I had a bone to pick with him and I felt sure the Secret Service would, too.

My uncle walked up just in time to hear the end of our conversation. "Did you say a reporter is here?" Uncle Laz looked around. He pulled off his apron and brushed the flour off of his pants. "How do I look?"

"What do you mean, how do you look?" I gave him a warning. "What does that matter?"

"I need to talk to him. Share a few things about my campaign. You know, Bella. Political stuff. Maybe he can help me get the word out about the Food Party."

I groaned but didn't bother to stop him. Uncle Laz headed the fellow's way and before long had him engaged in conversation. I couldn't be sure what my uncle was saying to him, but he got the fellow laughing.

I turned toward the bakery but before I could get there, Mama and Aunt Rosa approached.

"Bella-Bambina!" Mama wrapped me in a warm hug. "I didn't know you were coming to Parma Johns today. Rosa and I were just about to have lunch. Join us?"

"Maybe, but first I have to talk to Scarlet. And you two probably need to do something about Uncle Laz."

"Laz?" Rosa looked perplexed. "Where is he?"

"Talking to that reporter from the *New York Times*." I gestured and my aunt gasped.

"Reporter? What in the world?" She took off toward Laz, who had taken Mrs. Hightower's seat across from the reporter. Curious, I followed behind her. Mama tagged along on my heels. We got to the table just in time to hear Laz say something that made the fellow laugh.

"I'm just so sad that so many candidates are dropping out of the race," Laz added after the fellow calmed down.

"Why?" the reporter asked. "It narrows the field, which is good. On the democratic side they only have a handful of candidates. On the Republican side they've had, like, four hundred. It gets confusing when there are so many."

"Still, I hate to lose them as competition," Laz said. "I don't want my race to the White House to be too easy. I want people to know I won fair and square, not because some of the fellas gave up before their time. You know?"

Before long the entire Rossi clan had gathered around the reporter. How could I give this stranger a piece of my mind if my family members kept feeding him information? On the other hand, wouldn't it be better if I stayed 'on the down-low' as the Secret Service guys had said? Yes, I'd stay out of the guy's sightline and avoid his questions altogether.

One by one my parents and siblings shared their thoughts on the election and the candidates. I wanted to hide under a table as the squabbling began. Only Armando refrained from participating, stating that he wasn't registered to vote.

"Not registered to vote?" Rosa fanned herself. "Our children and grandchildren are going to read about this in their history books and it's up to us to determine what they read. If we don't engage in the process, then the ink on the pages won't come from our veins. We can't blame others if we don't vote."

"We joke around a lot," Mama said, "But voting is one of the rights we cherish the most. When I first came to this country with my parents, they celebrated when they got their cards to vote. I will never forget. Papa got in that line and waited his turn to cast his ballot for president of the United States. He was so happy. What an honor."

"Okay, okay, I'll register to vote." Armando rolled his eyes. "But I'm clueless about who to vote for."

"Why me, of course." Laz chuckled. "Haven't you figured it out yet, son? Your uncle is going to be the next president of the United States. It will be part of our Rossi legacy for the children and grandchildren to enjoy!" Laz rose and put his apron on as he headed toward the kitchen.

"We're going to leave a legacy for our kids, one way or the other," Mama said. "The question is, what sort of country do we want to place into their hands? What issues will we leave them to fix? What problems do we want to pass their way?" Great. Now she sounded like Earline.

"Well, when you put it like that. . ." He scratched his head. "Okay, okay. I'll vote for Uncle Laz."

"I wasn't really saying you should vote for Laz," Mama said. "Just vote your conscience. You'll have a little one soon, Armando, and then you'll understand. He'll grow up to be a man—"

"Woman."

"A woman?" My mother let out a squeal. "Really? Are you saying it's a baby girl? You're having a daughter?"

The reporter scribbled something in his notes.

"I. Am. So. Dead." My brother slapped his hand over his mouth and his eyes widened.

He was dead, all right. Scarlet would kill him for spilling the beans. Still, what happy news! A girl!

"Ooo, this is primo!" Mama did a little happy dance, right there in the aisle of Parma Johns. "A baby girl! You're having a girl! This is reason to celebrate. Oh, I just knew it! Go, team pink!"

"Who's having a girl?" Mayor Bradley asked as he approached the table. He looked my way and I could read the question mark in his eyes. I started coughing. After catching my breath I managed an emphatic. "No, not me!"

The mayor shifted his gaze to Armando. "You, Armando? Your baby is a girl?"

Before my brother could say a word, Mayor Bradley patted the reporter on the back. "Now here's a story for you, Mr. Jamison. Armando here is having a baby girl."

The reporter's eyes widened and his gaze shifted to my brother's rounded belly. "And I thought I wasn't going to get any good stories in Galveston." He snagged a pencil from behind his ear and scribbled something else in his notepad. "You're having a baby? Now, that *is* a story, especially in today's political climate."

"Why is that such a big story?" Armando asked. "Happens every day."

"Hardly." The guy scribbled down a few words and then peered into my brother's eyes with great intensity. "So, Armando—You did say your name was Armando, right?—When, exactly, did you realize you wanted to become a woman?"

Aunt Rosa let out a snort and then doubled over in laughter and Mama looked, well, mortified.

"A *woman*?" My brother slapped himself on the forehead. "I *don't* want to become a woman."

"It's nothing to be ashamed of. These days, it's perfectly normal."

"Um, not where I come from. And just for the record, never once in my life did I ever think about becoming a woman."

"That's not a hundred percent true," Mama said. "When you were a little boy you used to prance around the house in my high heeled shoes. And one time you dressed up in your sister's ballet outfit."

"Mama!" Armando looked horrified. "I was three."

"Seven," Mama countered. "But it was all in fun."

My brother turned to face the reporter. "I repeat—and I want this on the record—I have never had visions of becoming a woman. Or, of having a baby."

"Well, color me confused." The reporter grew silent and then appeared to have a light bulb moment. He snapped his finger. "Wait! I've got it! You're using a surrogate to carry your child."

"Surrogate?" Armando shook his head. "No idea what that is, but I don't need anything special to carry my own baby."

"So, you *are* pregnant, then?" The reporter went into a scribbling frenzy.

"No. And this is the craziest conversation I've ever had." Armando slapped himself on the forehead. "I mean, I know I've put on a few pounds— and I kid around all the time that I'm in my sixth month—"

"Sixth month?"

"But I'm not having a baby."

"But the mayor said you're—"

"Scarlet. *She's* having a baby."

"Scarlet is a surrogate?" The reporter asked.

Armando crossed his arms at his chest and glared at the man. "Stop. Calling. My. Wife. Names."

"Wait, she's your. . .wife?"

"Of course. And she's having a baby girl. Only, I'm not supposed to tell anyone any of that."

Mr. Jamison now wrote very slowly. "Rossi. Girl. No surrogate."

Oy vey.

The guy tapped his pencil on his notepad. "Hey, I think I met a Scarlet. She runs the bakery. She's pregnant?"

"Well, of course she's pregnant. That's what I've been trying to tell you. With a baby girl." Armando pinched his eyes shut and muttered, "Which is totally private information. I'm not supposed to be telling a soul until our Rossi family dinner on Friday night."

"Did you say you're one of the Rossis?" The reporter gave him a penetrating gaze.

"Yep." My brother nodded.

"Related to Lazarro, who's running for president as the Food Party candidate? I think I've got it all now. It's making sense to me."

I was glad it was making sense to somebody.

At this point Rosa got so tickled she couldn't stop laughing. The music overhead switched to *Mambo-Italiano*, which played loudly in the background.

"Laz is my uncle," Armando raised his voice to be heard above the music. "But he's not really running for office. He just has illusions of grandeur."

"Did you say he has delusions?" The reporter scribbled in his tablet. "Is he on medication?"

He wasn't. But I had a feeling we would all need some if this story hit the news.

"You Rossis are quite an interesting family," the reporter said. "But there's one family member I have yet to speak to."

"Who's that?' Armando called out above the music.

"Bella. Would you happen to know a Bella Rossi-Neeley?"

Oh. No. Please. No.

Everyone turned to look at me.

I took a little step backward.

"What do you need with my sister?" Armando asked.

"Oh, just hoping to ask her a few questions about the DeVine wedding."

I took another step backward. Then another. Then another. And then. . .I bumped into Uncle Laz, who happened to be walking behind me carrying a pitcher of soda to a nearby table. The pitcher shot out of his hand, sailed through the air, and landed all over the reporter's notepad.

I pinched my eyes shut and prayed for a clean get-away. Only when Laz hollered, "Bella-Bambina, *what* have you done?" did I realize there was no getting out of this one.

CHAPTER TEN

Love is Blue

Any American who is prepared to run for President should automatically, by definition, be disqualified from ever doing so.
Gore Vidal

I managed to somehow elude the reporter, though I heard from Mayor Bradley that he was staying at the Tremont and would be looking for me. That made my upcoming visit with Victoria even more nerve-wracking. She showed up at Club Wed on Thursday morning with the Agent O'Conner standing watch. Surely the Secret Serviceman could keep the big, bad reporter away.

As we walked through the lobby of Club Wed, I couldn't help but notice the sadness in the bride-to-be's eyes. I probably shouldn't have been so brave, but I came out and asked her, "What's wrong, Victoria? Please, tell me."

She stopped walking and shook her head, her eyes now brimming with tears. "My wedding is day after tomorrow, Bella." Victoria bushed away tears with the back of her hand.

"Yes, of course." I couldn't quite understand the tears, though. "Are you alright?"

She took a few steps through the reception hall without saying anything. When she turned to face me, the tears rushed down her cheeks. "I'm not, Bella. I'm not okay. Only, I don't know what to do about it. I'm marrying a man who's already married."

"Um. . . " I hardly knew what to say.

With the wave of a hand she appeared to dismiss any concerns. "Okay, so he's not married in the traditional sense, but he's married to his job. And by job, I mean his campaign. He's pinning all of his hopes on landing in the White House and sometimes I just have to wonder if I'm just a. . .a. . ."

A pretty wife-to-be who would look good hanging on his arm?

Thank goodness I didn't speak the words out loud, though they sailed through my brain with shocking clarity.

"I'm just a prop." She sighed and dropped into a chair. "A prop on his arm."

Okay, so I didn't need to say it. She'd done it for me.

Victoria leaned her elbows on the table and groaned aloud. "He wants a certain type of woman, Bella, and I guess I fit the bill. Well, not right at this very moment. He wouldn't be happy about my elbows on the table, but we're not in public, so what does it matter? I don't have to be perfect everywhere we go, right? I mean, no one's filming me now." She looked around, as if unsure.

I had to wonder, what with the *New York Times* reporter holed up at the Tremont. Was he hovering behind a bush?

"Surely there's more to your relationship than that." I took a seat next to her and gave her a sympathetic look. "Tell me how you met?"

"At a political rally."

Ah. So, maybe there wasn't more to it than that.

"A friend dragged me there kicking and screaming. Not my bag, if you get my drift. I didn't know much about politics, nor did I care. But I met Beau and fell hard."

"And Beau?"

"He fell hard, too. At least, I thought he did. He tells the story better than I do." A half-smile tipped up the edges of her lips. "Okay, so we really did hit it off. And everything was going fine. He was in his second term as senator and the media seemed to love the idea that he'd fallen in love."

"So, what's changed?" I asked.

"He has." She shook her head. "Well, I don't supposed he's really changed all that much. He's always been passionate about the things he believes in. And I'm passionate about them too. I just never saw myself as someone who was always in the public eye. What am I going to do if. . ." Her eyes widened and she looked as if she might be sick. "What if he's elected, Bella? I'll really be the first lady." She paled. "Like. . .*really* really. It won't be a maybe anymore."

"If that's what God has in your future then He will give you everything you need to fulfill the task."

"Even if it's a task I don't want?" She glanced around, as if anticipating an interruption from Beau. He wouldn't be joining us, of course. Not until the morning of the wedding. The man had another debate coming up.

"You're saying you don't want him to win?" I spoke the words in a whisper.

"Therein lies the conundrum. I love him and I want God's best for him. What if God's best is for Beau to be president of the United States? But what if

God's best for me is to be a soccer mom in Texas? You know? I just don't know if I can handle it, Bella. I don't."

"Can I ask you a question, Victoria?"

"Of course."

"If you could remove politics from the equation, would you love Beau any more. . .or any less?"

She began to sob in earnest now. In-between hiccoughs, she stammered, "I. . .I. . .I love him, no matter what."

"So, it's not really an issue of what he does or doesn't do. And by that, I'm not saying that what he's doing is easy. I realize it's hard."

"Very, very hard. And I don't mind admitting, sometimes I pray. . .sometimes I pray. . ."

"That he loses?" I asked.

She swiped at the back of her hand and whispered the word "Yes. And he's been down in the polls. Way down. So, losing feels like a real possibility now. I know it would devastate him but frankly, I—"

Off to the far side of the reception hall I saw Rosa fussing with the mop bucket. I knew she'd overheard our conversation, but she kept her thoughts to herself. For a while, anyway. By the time Victoria dissolved into a haze of tears, my aunt could no longer contain herself. She released her hold on the bucket and headed our way.

"Victoria?"

The bride-to-be paused from her tears to look up. "Y-yes?" She sniffled.

Rosa took her by the hand. "I know we've only known one another a short while, so I hope what I'm about to say isn't presumptuous. Bella can vouch for me. I speak my mind but I do it prayerfully."

"O-okay." I could see the doubt in Victoria's eyes. Still, I knew better than to interrupt my aunt when she was on a roll.

Rosa took a chair and sat next to the teary-eyed bride. "There was a time," my aunt explained, "when my relationship with Laz was much more complicated. For many years we barely got along."

"You and Laz?" Victoria looked stunned. "You two are perfect for each other. Like. . .peanut butter and jelly. Mozzarella and garlic."

"Hardly." Rosa laughed. "Anyway, Bella can back me up on this—Laz and I were two people going two separate ways. The bickering was endless. I think we were both afraid of what a relationship would look like between two very different people. He was set in his ways, I was set in mine."

"Ah." Victoria nodded. "I see."

"The truth is, a good marriage will be able to weather the differences. I learned this first-hand. I'm not saying everything is perfect. We still have our days when the differences between us feel like the Grand Canyon. But I love that old man more than life itself, and I dare say there's coming a day—maybe forty years from now—when you'll be sitting with some scared young bride telling her something similar. Things might be frightening. You might not know if this wedding should move forward, but if you put God at the center of it all—and I know you will—you and Beau will be an old married couple with stories to tell."

Before she could respond, Victoria's cell phone rang. She pulled it from her purse and her eyes widened when she saw the number. "It's Beau." She quickly cleared her throat and then answered with a bright, happy voice. "Hey, baby." She rose and began to pace the room. I could tell within a minute or two that the news from his end wasn't good, but I didn't want to eavesdrop, so I stood and took a few steps out of the reception hall and into the kitchen with Rosa tagging along behind me. Several minutes later Victoria located us. She shoved the phone back into her purse and gave me a woeful look. "Bella, I feel awful."

"About what?" I asked.

"The latest polls just came out and Beau's numbers have dropped again. . .a lot." She shoved her phone in her purse and her shoulders slumped forward. "It's my fault."

"It's not your fault, Victoria. You know that. People can put their trust in polls, anyway."

"He just sounds so. . .dejected." She released a little sigh. "I'm so torn. I want the man I love to be happy. Being President will make him happy. But it will make me miserable."

I wanted to respond, but something caught my attention. Just beyond the window, a strange shadow, followed by a fast-moving object. What in the world?

"B-Bella, what's happening?"

Before I could respond, the glass in the window shattered. I shot under the table and pulled Rosa down with me. Victoria landed on top of us and we all laid there, completely silent, our breaths hard and fast.

Agent O'Conner was in the room before either of us dared speak. "My men got him, Miss Brierley," his booming voice rang out. "You have nothing to worry about."

"G-G-Got *who*?" Victoria remained on the floor in the fetal position.

"Some guy claiming to be a reporter. We've got him handcuffed and headed to jail. He was just outside the kitchen window."

"Listening in?" Victoria looked panicked at this idea.

"Nope. He had just slipped in front of the window and my guys lunged at him. He won't be reporting anything for a while. So, you're safe." He extended his hand and helped Victoria up, then did the same for me.

I couldn't stop shaking. If this was a pre-cursor to the upcoming wedding, I'd bow out right now, thank you very much.

From the look on Victoria's face, she might bow out, too. I had a feeling this incident was just the icing on the cake for a bride who was already having very, very cold feet.

CHAPTER ELEVEN
I Just Called to Say I Love You

It is necessary for me to establish a winner image. Therefore, I have to beat somebody.
Richard M. Nixon

On Saturday morning I awoke with a knot in my stomach. This week had provided enough drama for the rest of the year. From the minute the *New York Times* reporter landed in jail, other journalists—if one could call them that—had swarmed the island. Thanks to the Secret Service, Club Wed was now the safest place to be. I had round-the-clock surveillance, and they would remain until the end of tomorrow evening's event.

Of course, we had to get through another event today before thinking ahead. This morning's wedding reception would be a breeze in comparison to tomorrow's soiree. But, turning the reception hall over in just a few hours would be nerve-wracking. We'd have to go from a red and gold Italian themed reception for fifty to a full out Victorian tea party for three hundred. I shivered, just thinking about it.

Then again, maybe the shivering was caused by something else. "D.J.?" I poked him and he stirred in the bed. "D.J., is it extra-cold in here or something?"

My hubby stirred in the bed and then rolled over. "It is cold. Brr." He pulled the covers over his head and fell back asleep, his gentle snores taking over.

Okay, then. I'd have to figure this one out on my own. I slipped out from under the covers, my feet landing on the cold, wood floor. Ack. I sprinted as fast as my early-morning feet would allow, all the way to the thermostat. I rubbed my eyes to make out the number: 59. W-what? Fifty-nine degrees inside the house?

I messed around with the thermostat for a couple of minutes to make sure I'd set the dumb thing properly. I had. Looked like this was a job for D.J.. Only, he was still curled up in bed.

"Mama?" I glanced down to see Rosie standing in the hallway behind me. "I'm c-c-c-cold!"

"Me too, honey."

"The twins are crying."

I strained to make out the sound. Sure enough, Holly and Ivy's faint cries sounded from their bedroom upstairs.

I leaned down and gave Rosie a kiss. "Mama will take care of the babies. Will you go wake up daddy?"

"Wake up daddy!" She let out a squeal and bounded toward the master bedroom. D.J. might not be happy to be awakened but who could resist such a darling little girl?

I got the twins from their cribs and bundled them in sweaters and their heaviest leggings then went back downstairs. Tres joined us, wrapped in his Ninja Turtles blanket, and we ate a fast breakfast that included hot oatmeal and cocoa. Anything to warm us up. Afterwards D.J. stayed with the kids while I dressed for today's event and then headed off to Club Wed.

I arrived at the wedding facility at ten-fifteen and gave the building a final once-over before today's reception commenced. Their ceremony was probably underway at St. Patrick's right now. Pam and Fred—the sweetest elderly couple I'd ever met—would soon be Mr. and Mrs. Grantham. They should arrive at Club Wed no later than eleven. Even Agent O'Conner, who stood watch while I worked, seemed to know all of the details.

Sure enough, the wedding guests started pouring in at ten minutes till eleven. The wedding party entered the reception hall at exactly eleven o'clock. The bride and groom—both in their 70s—looked blissfully happy. And relaxed. In other words, the polar opposite of Beau and Victoria. Not that I needed to be comparing anyone.

With Mama and Pop's help I stayed on task. Mr. And Mrs. Grantham had a short but sweet reception and their guests, mostly elderly folks, left after just an hour and a half. Time to flip this place in preparation for tomorrow's reception. For whatever reason, the idea left my stomach in knots.

Or maybe the knots had something to do with not eating lunch. Ugh. I'd have to grab some leftovers from wedding #1.

A quick trip to the kitchen was in order. I located a tray of chicken salad sandwiches and dove right in.

By one o'clock it was all-hands-on-deck as D.J., Nick, Pop, Armando, Joey and my nephews arrived to bring in more tables. Sophia, Mama, Rosa and I flew into action, putting the tablecloths in place. Tomorrow I would officially set the tables with the gorgeous plates we'd rented and with the centerpieces Cassia was bringing, but for today this would have to do. When we finished in the reception hall I headed to the chapel to make sure everything was in order for tonight's rehearsal.

Weariness took its hold on me and I sat in the front pew to think through my plans—both for tonight's rehearsal and tomorrow's ceremony and reception. I must've fallen asleep. D.J.'s gentle voice roused me from a peaceful slumber.

"Bella?"

"Hmm?"

"You sleeping?"

"Who, me?" I sat up and wiped the drool from the corners of my mouth. "Um, I don't know. Was I?"

"Mm-hmm." He slipped his arm over my shoulders. "And I don't blame you. You can snooze a little longer if you like, but why don't you go to your parents' place? Sleep in a real bed."

"What if I slept through tonight's rehearsal?" I sat up straight, the very idea terrifying me. "And what about the kids?"

"Marcella just called to say she's taken them to the Aquarium."

"Wow, she's brave."

"Yep. But she didn't seem to mind a bit. So, head next door and sleep a couple of hours. I promise to wake you up by five. How does that sound?"

"Too good to be true."

The next two hours were spent in a warm bed. In a warm house. D.J. woke me up at five o'clock, as promised, and I did my best to make myself look presentable, then headed next door to the wedding facility, where I found Agent O'Conner gabbing with the Splendora sisters.

The Splendora sisters? What were they doing here?

"Bella!" Twila extended her arms. "Come and give me a hug, honey-bun."

I gave Agent O'Conner a "What in the world?" look and he grinned. "We ran background checks on these three weeks ago. An informant tipped us off that they might make an appearance."

"An informant?"

"Your husband, Mrs. Neeley. Your husband. He said they like to come and go from Club Wed."

"Oh, we do." Jolene giggled. "We come to Club Wed. . .a lot."

"And we hate to go," Bonnie Sue added. "It's always so hard to leave."

"And to think, we met this wonderful young man." Twila gave O'Conner an admiring smile then pinched his cheek. "He was just telling us about his wife and kids. Did you know he's got twins, too, Bella?"

I looked at O'Conner, stunned. "You do?"

"Yeah." He pulled out photos and I had to laugh when I saw they were both girls.

"We have more in common than we knew." Strange, how the Splendora sisters had managed to get this much out of him, though. Then again, they had a gift for drawing information out of people.

O'Conner started telling a story about his kids. Just a couple minutes into the tale, Victoria arrived, dressed in a gorgeous designer dress, beautiful heels and perfect hair and makeup. What a shame, that Beau would never get to see her all dolled up on her wedding rehearsal night. O'Conner startled to attention and put the pictures of his kids away and excused himself to join the other agents outside. I thought Twila, Bonnie Sue and Jolene would take the hint and follow him, but they stayed put.

Victoria gave me a little wave and walked toward us. "Hey, Bella."

"Victoria!" I walked over and gave her a hug. "It's rehearsal day."

"Yes." She offered a strained smile. "Rehearsal day."

Jolene took a couple of steps toward Victoria, her finger outstretched. "Why, I'd know you anywhere. You're that pretty young thing who's gonna marry our senator, Beauregard DeVine. I've seen you on TV. And I saw *him* on the news just this morning. Is this the big day?"

"Tomorrow," Victoria said. "It's such a shame that he's got the debate tonight and will have to miss the wedding rehearsal. But we'll do the best we can without him."

"Oh, Bella!" Bonnie Sue clamped a hand over her mouth. "Is *this* the big surprise wedding you couldn't tell us about? The one that was so hush-hush?" She giggled. "Guess the cat's out of the bag now, eh?"

"Where have you been, Bonnie Sue?" Twila rolled her eyes. "It's been all over the news for two days, ever since that reporter fella got arrested." She looked at Victoria. "He didn't do you any harm, did he, sweet girl?"

"No. I never even saw him. He was outside of the window."

"Trying to sneak in, I dare say." Twila fanned herself. "Terrible antics. Those reporters will do anything for a story. Ask me how I know."

"How do you know?" Victoria asked.

"I'm the mayor of Splendora. And the paparazzi drove me crazy during my run for office."

"Paparazzi." Bonnie Sue rolled her eyes. "Puh-leeze. One lame reporter from the Splendora Gazette is hardly paparazzi."

"Well, anyway, the whole thing put such a strain on my nerves. And don't even get me started on the toll it took on my marriage. Running for office ain't for sissies. A hundred percent of it was my doing. I got a little, um, shall we say. . ."

"Puffed up," Bonnie Sue chimed in. "Her head blew up bigger than her backside and I think we can all agree that's a tremendous amount of inflation."

Victoria clamped a hand over her mouth, likely to keep from laughing.

"You're a fine one to talk, Bonnie Sue." Twila put her hands on her ample hips and glared at her friend. "Did you or did you not tell me just this very morning that you put on ten pounds over the holiday season?"

"Nine pounds, but that's beside the point." Bonnie Sue rolled her eyes. "At any rate, Twila thought she was all that and a bag of chips,"

"Ooo, chips." Jolene licked her lips. "But Twila can't deny it's true. For a while there she started to believe her own press."

Twila released a sigh. "I guess what they're trying to say here is, I went through a season where I let my ego run away with me. But I have since repented. And God has not only given me the job of mayor, He's managed to strengthen my relationship with my hubby. And I dare say he'll give you a strong marriage too."

"Can I ask a question?" Victoria's forehead wrinkled as she spoke. "Woman to woman?"

"Well sure, honey."

"When you were running for office, did your emotions go up and down like a roller-coaster?"

"Every day! My emotions ran hot and cold," Twila explained. "When I thought I might win, I was happy and carefree. When I suspected I might lose, I became sullen and cross. I let the process dictate my emotions."

"That's exactly what's happening now. Poor Beau. The polls are out and his numbers are down, so he's plummeted into despair. Our wedding is tomorrow. We should be the happiest two people on the planet. I'm starting to think. . ." She paused. "I'm starting to think we should post-pone the wedding until after he wins. . .or loses."

"If it makes you feel any better, he's got my vote." Jolene said. "I'm as conservative as they come."

"Unless you count her Lady Clairol hair coloring and that crazy low-cut blouse she wore to the Christmas banquet at church. It was anything but conservative." Bonnie Sue gave her a knowing look. "And some would argue that your hot pink lip-liner borders on liberal, too."

"I do *not* have liberal lip-liner." Jolene put her hands on her hips.

"Do too," Bonnie Sue countered.

"Do not," Jolene argued. She reached in her purse and came out with her compact, which she flipped open. Seconds later, she was examining her lips.

At this point, Twila stepped between them. "Ladies, this is Victoria's wedding rehearsal day and nothing is going to spoil it."

"Not even a missing groom?" the bride asked, her countenance sad.

"Not even a missing groom." Twila looped her arm through Victoria's. "Now come with me, you pretty thing. Let's get you to the chapel on time. And don't you fret. I have it on good authority—she pointed up to the ceiling—that the Lord is about to perform a miracle."

That certainly got my attention. If Twila believed God was going to perform a miracle. . .well, I wanted to be a first-hand witness.

CHAPTER TWELVE
Because You Loved Me

My brother Bob doesn't want to be in government - he promised Dad he'd go straight.
John F. Kennedy

On the night of the wedding rehearsal everyone showed up. . .except the groom. Okay, so we knew in advance he wouldn't be there, what with the big debate on CBS that same night. He was right where any presidential candidate would be on such a night—with his opponents bickering over the finer points of how to save the country from ruin. Only, I had a feeling his absence wouldn't exactly save his bride-to-be's heart from pain.

At seven o'clock we started by getting the wedding party in place—the groomsmen would enter from the front and the bridesmaids from the back. But first I had to give instructions to the grandparents, parents, flower girl and ring bearer. It took a few minutes to situate everyone, but by seven fifteen we were ready to do our first run-through. Twila took it upon herself to help with the children while Bonnie Sue busied herself gabbing with the parents of the bride. Jolene worked with D.J. and Armando in the sound booth. Or maybe she just wanted to hang out with O'Conner, who seemed to be enjoying her antics.

At the very last minute, though, something occurred to me. "I usually have someone stand in for the bride," I explained. "But in this case, maybe it'd make more sense to have someone stand in for the groom."

Victoria's father offered to do so, but she nixed that idea. "Feels too weird—marrying my own dad. Any other takers?"

"I'll do it." The best man raised his hand. "Beau's my best friend. I don't think he'd mind."

I somehow managed to get the entire wedding party through the process of moving into place in front of the pastor, though my focus kept shifting back and forth from the bride-to-be to the Secret Service guys at the back. One of them—the guy with the mole—was leaning over the soundboard, querying D.J. about something.

Focus, Bella. Focus!

I shifted my attention back to Victoria and the bridal party. "Okay, pastor. . .now it's your turn. Do your thing."

He led them through the ceremony, all smiles. Just about the time he got to the "you may now kiss the bride" part, a voice rang out from the back of the chapel.

"I'll take over now if you don't mind. Don't think I want my best friend kissing my girl."

We all turned to discover the groom had arrived, looking a bit disheveled.

Victoria let out a squeal. "Beau-Beau! You made it!"

"I made it."

At this point the whole room came alive. Victoria's parents looked stunned. For that matter, so did Beau's mother, who had been relatively silent. Bonnie Sue and Jolene did a happy dance and Twila stood at the front of the room, arms lifted in praise. "I knew it!" she hollered. "Praise the Lord! I knew a miracle was on its way. Thank You, Jesus. You've answered our prayers!"

He'd answered them, all right, but I still didn't understand.

The happy bride rushed down the aisle toward her groom and gave him half a dozen kisses, then stopped suddenly. "Wait. . .what about the debate?"

"Debate? What debate?" He winked. "Who needs a little old debate, anyway? They're highly overrated."

"Are you saying you skipped it?"

He nodded. "Yep. I skipped it. Caught a flight back to Texas instead." He glanced my way and shrugged. "Bella, do you mind if I say a little something before we carry on with the rehearsal?"

"Please," I said. "Be my guest."

He gestured for the others to take a seat and then stood at the front of the room. Even the pastor took a seat, now looking more like a congregant ready to hear a sermon.

And what a sermon it turned out to be. Beau started by apologizing to his bride for nearly ruining their wedding rehearsal. Then he apologized to everyone in attendance for letting his political ambitions get in the way of his personal life.

Out of the corner of my eye I watched as Twila listened to his every word, tears streaming from her eyes.

After making apologies, Beau gestured for Victoria to join him at the front of the room. "I think I've been trying to prove something to myself." His words were directed at her, but he spoke loud enough for all to hear.

"What's that, baby?" she asked.

"That I'm a winner." He paused and his expression grew sad. "My whole life I felt like I was never good enough."

"What do you mean?"

"I mean some people. . .always saw me as a loser."

His mother stood and faced him head-on. "You're talking about your father, aren't you?"

Beau nodded. "Yes. And even though he's been gone over ten years, I've been trying to prove something to him. His admiration and respect was all I really craved. But it occurred to me today, no matter how hard I try, even if I win the ultimate prize and sit in the Oval Office, he won't be there to witness it. And you know what? It's not really his love I need, anyway." He turned to face Victoria. "It's yours." Beau swept his happy bride into his arms. "Yours. . .and God's. And I already know I have His."

"I hope you know you have mine, too," she whispered.

"I don't deserve it. I've neglected you. I've put my own needs above yours."

"You've put the needs of a country ahead of mine," she countered. "And somehow I found that forgivable every step of the way. So, please stop worrying, okay?"

"My worries are behind me." He kissed her on the forehead. "But I've learned a lot about what it's going to take to keep them behind me. This morning the Lord reminded me of a scripture: What does it profit a man if he wins the White House but forfeits his soul?" He paused and gave a little shrug. "Okay, so that's not exactly how it goes, but it's close. How would it benefit me to win the highest prize in the land—the office of President—if I lost my soul along the way?"

"You won't lose your soul, baby." Victoria threw her arms around him. "I know you better than that."

"Maybe not completely, but if you knew the countless hours I've spent fretting, strategizing, calculating. . .worrying. . .you would know that I've already given too much of myself to this process."

"Your motives are noble, though."

My motives might've been noble in the beginning but lately they've been slipping. I've cared more about numbers, more about the money coming in from my supporters, than what a win would actually mean for the country. And for you."

"What are you saying, Beau?" Her forehead wrinkled in concern.

"What I should've said weeks ago. I hope you don't mind that I plan to do so now in front of our friends and family." He turned to face the crowd and the room grew silent. "I plan to withdraw from the race, effective today. That's what I've been trying to say all along."

"W-what?" Victoria paled. "Are you sure?"

"I am. From tomorrow on, I'm all yours. Well, yours and the state of Texas. But my term will be over soon and I'll probably pull back from politics altogether. Maybe go back into law."

"Whoa, there." She shook her head. "I love the fact that you're a public servant, so don't throw the baby out with the bath water. If you're convinced you should withdraw from the run for the White House, I will agree wholeheartedly. But let's don't think about leaving Texas without the best senator they've ever had. That's an unnecessary move."

"I'll pray about it, I promise."

"Oh, praise the Lord!" Jolene raised her arms to the sky. "I couldn't bear it if I lost my favorite senator."

He gave Jolene a "Who in the world are you?" look, then continued. "Well, like I said, I'll pray about it. And that's really the driving force in my life right now. A combination of things led me to drop out of the presidential race: the polls showed me slipping off of the radar, but even that wasn't what got to me. I really felt like I needed to bow out because, well. . ." He raked his fingers through his hair.

"Why?" we all asked in unison.

"Because I had a Damascus Road experience last night."

Laz paled. "Oh. My. Goodness. Did it involve a bus? Headlights?"

"No." Beau shook his head. "No bus. No headlights. Nothing weird. I was in bed last night, nearly asleep, when I—"

"Saw a bright light?" Laz asked.

"Well, that too. The power had been off—some sort of electrical problem in the hotel—and it came back on just as I was dozing off. The whole room lit up. But the strangest part. . .the TV came on. I was blinded by the light but I heard the voice on the television, loud and clear."

"What did the voice say?" Mama asked.

"Yes, tell us, baby," Victoria said.

He nodded and his eyes narrowed. "The voice said, 'Turn and go the other way.'"

"Turn and go the other way?" we all repeated in unison.

"Was it. . .God?" Twila asked. "Speaking through the TV?"

Beau shook his head. "No. It turned out the television was on a rerun of Gilligan's Island. It was the Skipper, telling Gilligan to turn and go the other way so he wouldn't fall into quicksand. But, just as plain as day, it was the Lord speaking to me. 'Turn and go the other way.'"

"The Lord certainly speaks in mysterious ways." Bonnie Sue shook her head and tears started to flow. "Thank You, Jesus!"

"Yes, He certainly does." Beau looked at Bonnie Sue, and though it was obvious he didn't have a clue who she was, he gave her a polite nod. "And now, friends and family, I think it's time for a wedding rehearsal, don't you?"

"Oh I do! I do!" Victoria threw her arms around his neck and planted kisses on his cheek.

"Don't say your I Do's too quickly, girlie," Twila said. "Or you'll end up hitched a day too early."

"I wouldn't mind one little bit." Victoria giggled. "Not one little bit."

She might not mind, but I sure would, and so would tomorrow's guests. They were looking forward to a tea party wedding, and I planned to give it to them. In fact, this might just be the best wedding anyone in the great state of Texas had ever seen!

CHAPTER THIRTEEN
I Will Always Love You

Every politician should have been born an orphan and remain a bachelor.
Lady Bird Johnson

Valentine's morning dawned clear and bright, though very, very cold. And though we'd worked our tails off last night to get Club Wed set up for today's big event, I found myself fretting.

D.J. and I got the kiddos ready for church and hit the road for the early service. I didn't stay for Sunday school, not with my thoughts in such a whirl. I headed off to the wedding facility to give things a final once-over. I couldn't help but think back to last night's announcement from the groom. I could feel the tension leave Victoria's face the moment Beau told her he was dropping out of the race. Surely today's ceremony and reception would be a breeze, now that their life-stresses were behind them.

Of course, mine were just beginning. I still had to coordinate a wedding with three hundred guests. And deal with the Secret Service. Even though Beau was no longer a candidate, they still planned to make their presence known. And make it known, they did.

As I entered the wedding facility, O'Conner gave me a wave, which I returned. A couple of the other guys nodded at me, then shifted their gaze to the road, as if expecting a calamity of some sort. Me? My expectations were completely different. I had a feeling in my gut that this would be a wonderful day, all the way around.

As soon as I entered the reception hall I went to work unloading the china plates I'd rented. Cassia put the centerpieces in place. A few minutes later Sophia arrived to help. "Um, Bella?"

"Yes?" I looked up from my work.

"Are my eyes deceiving me, or is there a man in a suit on the roof of the building holding a pair of binoculars?"

I sighed. "Kind of takes away the romance, when you put it like that, but yes, there's a man in a suit on the roof. And I would imagine he's holding binoculars."

"Do you mind if I ask why there's a man on the roof holding binoculars?"

"He's keeping watch over his flock by night."

"Very funny. So, Secret Service, then?"

"Yeah."

"But the groom dropped out of the race. Right? I mean, I wasn't here last night to hear it for myself, but it's all over the news."

"Yeah, he dropped out, but they're still covering him. From what I was just told, he might be more of a risk after making the announcement. You never know what weirdos might be out there, ready to pounce."

"Lovely. Very comforting idea."

"I'm sure it'll be okay. I feel better those guys are here to keep a watchful eye on things."

Before long Rosa arrived. Then Laz. Then Mama. Then Pop. Before long, the whole crew was there, taking care of last minute details. I kept up my work at the table, putting each lovely piece of china in place. Renting these gorgeous pieces had been a terrific idea, if I did say so, myself.

"Oooh, Bella!" Sophia held up a dinner plate, her mouth dropping open. "This is magnificent."

"I think so too. You should've seen the price tag attached." I shivered, remembering. "But the bride wanted true Victorian pieces that looked as if they'd come straight out of the late 1800s, so that's what she's getting. I can only pray no one drops a plate. Not sure you'd believe me if I told you the replacement cost on even one piece."

Her hand began to tremble and she set the plate on the table. "Maybe I'd better let you and Mama do this. You know what a Klutz I am. Is there something else I can help you with?"

I directed her to Cassia, who needed her help with the centerpieces. Minutes later, Scarlet arrived with the cake—each layer still in individual boxes. Rosa helped her assemble the gorgeous six-tiered wonder and we all gathered around as Scarlet took out a large box of flowers she'd crafted by hand—all from gumpaste and fondant—and applied them in cascade-form down the cake. I'd never seen such a beautiful, elegant combination of flowers, or such delicate scrolling.

"Whoa, Scarlet." I gave a little whistle. "I think this one's pretty enough for a—"

"First lady?" she asked and then gave me a wink.

"Ah, you didn't hear, then?" Rosa cleared a blob of buttercream from the tablecloth and then gathered up the leftover crumbs into one of the boxes. "DeVine dropped out of the race."

"No." Scarlet's expression shifted from joy to despair. "Seriously?"

"Yep." I gave a nod. "You sound disappointed, but the bride sure isn't. She's relieved."

"Ah." Scarlet grew silent. "I can't believe I didn't hear about it."

"It's been on every news station," Mama said.

"I was at the bakery most of the night finishing up the cake." She yawned. "That might explain it. I guess it's just pure ego on my part. I wanted to be able to say that I'd made the wedding cake for the president and his wife. You know? Sure would've looked good on my resume."

"Hey, he's still a senator who ran for president," I reminded her. "There's got to be something special that can come from that story. The man who would be president, and all that. . ."

"Yeah, I guess. Only, you wouldn't believe how much trouble I went to. I talked several of my customers into voting for him. I've been working overtime to get him elected." She grew quiet and then shrugged. "Oh well. Dumb move on my part, I guess."

"Only dumb if you hadn't planned to vote for him in the first place," Rosa said, and then gave Scarlet a wink. "But we won't ask you that question."

"Actually. . ." Scarlet took the box of crumbs from Rosa. "Ah, never mind. I guess it doesn't matter now." She stood back and examined the cake. "But it does look pretty, doesn't it? I've never made one that I liked more. Did you notice how intricate the piping is?"

"I did. But what really takes my breath away are the flowers, Scarlet. I hope you won't take this the wrong way, but you've really come a long way, baby. I mean, you were always good, but your flowers are really life-like now."

"Girl, you wouldn't believe how many hours I spent working on those. This little bambina and I have had a lot of quiet time in the kitchen." She rubbed her belly.

"So, Armando told you that we already know the baby's sex?" I asked.

She nodded. "Yeah. I don't mind. I mean, we planned to do a gender reveal cake next weekend at our Rossi family dinner, but what does it matter, really? As long as we all welcome her in style at my baby shower. You are helping with that, right, Bella?" She gave me an imploring look.

"Helping? You bet I am. Wouldn't miss that for anything in the world." I gave her a hug and she seemed to relax.

A couple of minutes later I noticed O'Conner standing guard near the cake table. He watched as Scarlet put the finishing touches on the confectionary masterpiece. I couldn't help myself. I walked up to him and patted him on the back. "Have time for a little lighthearted conversation, Agent O'Conner?"

"We don't do lighthearted conversation, Mrs. Neeley."

"Right, I know. Just kidding."

"We don't kid, Mrs. Neeley."

"Know that, too." I gave him a little wink. "Do you mind if I ask one question, though?"

"Ask away."

"Why do you guys always assume the position?"

"Assume the position?" He looked perplexed. "I beg your pardon?"

"You guys always stand in the same position. All of you. Hands clasped together. Standing perfectly still. You know. . .the position. And all of your guys seems to be really. . ."

"Buff," Scarlet said, looking away from the cake for a moment. "They're buff."

Scarlet!" I gave her a "Please be quiet" look but that didn't stop her.

"We work hard to stay in shape, Ma'am: Boxing. Wrestling. Weight training. Jiu-Jitsu."

"Jiu-Jitsu?" Scarlet took one of the wedding cookies from a tray and started nibbling on it. "Is that some kind of religious cult?"

"No Ma'am." O'Conner cleared his throat and turned to face another direction.

Scarlet leaned in close. "I had no idea these guys had their own separate religion," she whispered. "Have you ever heard of Jiu-Jitsu, Bella?"

"Yes, but it's not a religion."

"He seems pretty dedicated to it." She finished off the cookie.

"Um, Scarlet?" I pointed to the crumbs on her fingertips.

"Oops. Almost forgot they weren't meant for me. But don't worry, Bella. . .I made plenty of extras. I always do. Besides, I'm pregnant. You know? A girl needs her cookies when she's expecting."

"Then what's my excuse?" Pop asked as he walked by and snagged one.

When I scolded him, he pushed out his belly to make himself look pregnant.

"I'm not falling for that," I said. "Now, everyone back away from the table. I need everything to be perfect today."

"Things will never be perfect, Bella-Bambina." Mama's voice sounded from behind me. I turned to face her. "But we do the best we can. True?"

"True. I just want this to be a memorable day."

"Oh, trust me. . .it'll be memorable." Pop rolled his eyes. "When I crossed the lawn from our house to the wedding facility, a Secret Service agent patted me down. Trust me when I say this is a day I'll never forget." He rolled his eyes. "And I'll also add that it can't end soon enough for me."

From across the room I caught a glimpse of Uncle Laz trying to hand out *Laz for Prez* buttons to a couple of the caterers. One of them took his button and pinned it on her apron, but O'Conner made her remove it.

"Laz isn't giving up, is he?" I groaned. "He's going to carry this joke all the way—"

"To the White House." Uncle Laz said as he stepped into place beside me. "So, you might as well wear one of my buttons, Bella. You know you want to."

"I'm sorry, Uncle Laz, but I can't do that, especially not today. You know that."

"Sure you can. DeVine has dropped out of the race. That ups my chances."

"From .000001%, you mean?" Pop slapped his knee and laughed. He somehow choked on a cookie as he did. For a minute there I thought we were going to have to do the Heimlich. So did O'Conner, who came running. Fortunately, Pop managed to catch his breath.

And just in time, too. I glanced at my watch and gasped as I realized the bride was expected to arrive any minute now. I sprinted to her changing room to make sure every detail was in order. Then, just as I turned back toward the door, Victoria swept in, entourage in tow.

Yep, it was time to get this show on the road.

CHAPTER FOURTEEN
Endless Love

You begin saving the world by saving one man at a time; all else is grandiose
romanticism or politics.
Charles Bukowski

At five minutes after seven on the evening of Sunday, February 14th, I stood at
the back of the Club Wed chapel and watched as our most famous bride made
her entrance up the aisle. Okay, so I was framed on both sides by Secret
Service guys, but they didn't intimidate me or jar me from my current role as
wedding coordinator. I kept a watchful eye on the bridal party, perfectly lined
up at the front of the church, and got a little teary-eyed as Victoria's father
gave her away.

At this point I leaned against the wall, exhausted but energized as I
watched every minute of the ceremony. Though last night's rehearsal was a
bit crazy, the groom missing most of it, everything came off without a hitch
this time around. And even though the bride hadn't had much time to give to
the décor, the flowers, the columns, the tulle, the twinkling lights, or even the
ornate candelabras, she seemed completely content in her surroundings.

Me? I thought the chapel looked prettier than I'd ever seen it. I'd never
given thought to turning it into a Victorian picture-postcard, but the
transformation left me breathless.

Turned out I wasn't the only one who was breathless. The Secret Service
guy to my right lunged forward to snatch a cell phone out of the hand of a
woman attempting to take a photograph. Poor gal never saw it coming. She let
out a gasp but willingly gave up the cell phone then clamped her lips together
and turned to face the front of the chapel. Thank goodness few others noticed.

Wowza, these security guys took their job seriously.

I took mine seriously, too. At the very moment the reverend pronounced
the couple husband and wife, I sprang into action. I opened the back doors of
the chapel so that Mr. and Mrs. DeVine could pass through, and I gave Victoria
the biggest smile in the world. . .which she returned. Before she kissed her
husband. And kissed him again.

The kissing went on as the guests were ushered out of the chapel and
directed to the reception hall for appetizers, which they would enjoy while

the wedding party had photos taken. I quickly connected with the photographer, gave her a few last-minute instructions, then headed to the reception hall to make sure things there were running smoothly.

I entered to a full house. The caterers had already set out the appetizers and guests formed lines to fill their plates. Mama gave me a little wave from the kitchen door and I took a few steps in her direction, pausing only to glance at the soundboard where my brother and D.J. would soon take up residence.

Mama wiped her hands on her apron and gestured to Rosa and Laz, who couldn't seem to remember that they didn't need to be helping the caterers. "What do you think, Bella? It's beautiful, isn't it?"

"Mm-hmm. Looks heavenly. Very. . .Valentiney."

"I think the bride will love it."

"Honestly? I think the bride is so distracted by her husband's decision not to run for president that she won't notice. But the guests seem to be enjoying it, and that's what matters."

"Speaking of people dropping out of the race. . ." Mama gestured with her head to Uncle Laz, who now filled a teapot with hot water. "Did you hear?"

"No." I shook my head.

"He's decided to stop the shenanigans. No more signs in the front yard. No more posters at the restaurant. I think his decision had something to do with DeVine's passionate speech at the rehearsal last night. It really got to him."

"Wow, that was quick. Just a couple of hours ago he was trying to pin a *Laz for Prez* button on me."

"I guess he came to his senses." Mama shrugged. "Either that, or Rosa knocked some sense into him."

I gave my uncle a sympathetic look. "Well, for what it's worth, I think Laz would've made a great President. The country would've been well-fed, at any rate."

"And I dare say Aunt Rosa would've made a great first lady." Mama gave her sister a warm smile. "Though, to be honest, I don't know how they could've handled it. They're so busy already. Between their TV show, Parma Johns and all of the weddings, they're overloaded."

"Yeah, what's up with all of that, anyway?" I asked. "I thought Laz was going to back away from Parma Johns and let Nick take over."

"You really fell for that? Your uncle is a workaholic, Bella. Rosa wants him to slow down, but I think he thrives on it."

Hmm. Well, I certainly understood what that was like.

I glanced over as D.J. and Armando took their places in the reception hall's sound booth. My sweet hubby gave me a little wink and then got to work. A couple of minutes later I lined the wedding party up in perfect order just outside the reception hall door and when D.J. announced them they made their grand entrance, couple by couple. When it came time to announce Mr. and Mrs. DeVine, the crowd came alive with cheers. I couldn't help but join in.

They took the time to greet their guests. In fact, I had a feeling it would be awhile before Victoria and Beau ate any of that fancy food the caterers had worked so hard on.

I looked on as they hugged and chatted with person after person. Mama joined me and let out a little whistle. "Man, that dress of hers is. . .wow." She paused and shook her head. "Did Gabi make that dress? It's remarkable!"

"Yes Ma'am. Custom-made. You don't even want to know how much it cost."

"Of course I do."

"Let's just say the lace is over a hundred years old, which is why it's got a bit of an ivory cast. You'll notice it's got tiny medallions of hand crocheted lace and inserts. Oh, and the pearls are real." I paused to give the bride a closer look. "I just love how those sheer lace sleeves fall over her shoulder like that, and how they loop under the arms."

"Yes. Really accentuates her hour-glass figure."

"It's lined in silk," I said. "And would you believe there are over fifty buttons up the back? You don't even want to know how long it took the bridesmaids to get them all buttoned."

"Or how long it's going to take Beau-Beau to *un*-button them." Mama giggled.

"True." I couldn't help but laugh in response to that. "Do you see how the gown has a slight bustle in the back?"

"Gorgeous," Mama said.

"From what I understand, that's the only part of the gown Victoria wasn't sure about. She was afraid it made her backside look big."

"My goodness, if you want to see a large backside, I would be happy to demonstrate what a real one looks like."

I looked over to see that Twila had joined us. "Um, no thank you," I said. "But thanks for the offer."

"I have to agree with your Mama," Twila said. "The gown is lovely."

"Everything is lovely," Jolene added with a happy sigh.

"Even the Secret Servicemen are lovely," Bonnie Sue added. "But please don't tell my husband I said that. He might get the wrong idea."

"Ooo, look at the bride's feet." Jolene let out a little squeal. "Are those. . .lace boots?"

"Ankle high," I explained. And yes, lace and soft pink suede. Dolce and Gabbana."

"How much?" Bonnie Sue asked.

"More than I make in a year as mayor, I'd be willing to bet." Twila sighed. "Oh, but what a way to spend a year's salary."

"That's Catania lace on those boots," Mama said. "I'd know it anywhere."

This led to a lengthy discussion about lace, which led to several comments from the ladies about vintage tea party décor, which led to a lengthy chat about the gorgeous wedding cake.

Wedding cake!

It was time to nudge the bride and groom toward the cake table for their first slice. Everyone in the room cheered as the once-bound-for-the-White-House groom shoved a piece of cake into his bride's face. They found equal delight when she returned the favor. Afterwards, the best man and maid of honor gave their speeches and toasts were made. Then the dance floor was opened.

I watched as D.J. and Armando manned the music, seamlessly weaving from one tune to the next. I found myself a little surprised to see that Beau-Beau was an excellent dancer—and not a shy one, either. He and Victoria spent a great deal of time in each other's arms on the dance floor.

The rest of the night seemed to sail by. I watched with a lump in my throat as the bride and groom thanked their guests, then I made sure Victoria's bag made it from the bride's changing room to their limousine. Finally, with the guests—and the Secret Service —looking on, the bride and groom climbed into the limo and headed off into the night, never looking back.

At this point the crowd began to dissipate. A few folks lingered, but most headed to their cars, all under the watchful eye of O'Conner and his men. Once we found ourselves alone in the reception hall, the Rossi family decided to partake of some of the leftovers.

"I don't know what most of this stuff is," D.J. said. "But it's not half bad."

Laz turned his nose up at much of it, but Rosa gave the trout a thumbs-up and Scarlet proclaimed the madeleines to be the best she'd ever eaten. We sat for some time, resting, and then reached that inevitable point where we knew we had to get to work clearing the room.

I buzzed along from table to table, removing the centerpieces. Then I went into the kitchen to make sure the caterers knew not to take any of the china place settings with them. Finally, I headed back out to the cake table, where I found O'Conner helping Scarlet and Armando box up the leftovers. I watched as he accidentally jabbed his fingers into the buttercream and then stuck them in his mouth.

"Mmm."

"Good, right?" Scarlet grinned.

"The best I've ever had."

She and Armando carried boxes of cake out to their van and I turned my attention to the Secret Serviceman. "Can I ask you a question, Agent O'Conner?"

"I'm off the clock. Right now I'm just Joe."

"Gee, I didn't know you guys went off the clock." I shrugged and snagged a couple of cookies, then handed one to him.

"So, off the record. . ." I leaned in to whisper the rest. "Who are you voting for? For president, I mean."

"I can't tell you that, Ma'am." He licked the cookie crumbs from his fingers.

"Sure you can. It's not top secret information, is it?"

"No. I can't tell you. . .because I haven't decided." He popped the rest of the cookie in his mouth and a delirious look came over him.

"Really? You mean you traveled all this time with DeVine and never planned to vote for him?"

O'Conner gave me a knowing look. "*You* planned his wedding and I suspect you never intended to vote for him, either."

I sighed. "True, that. There are a lot of other candidates to consider."

"Yep. I will add that I've tasted your uncle's cooking and am leaning heavily in his direction."

"I'm sad to tell you he's pulled out of the race."

"Many a good man has."

"So, you had planned to be a Food Party voter?" I asked as I reached for a cookie.

"Maybe."

"How would your Jui-Jitsu friends have reacted?" I took a bite of the cookie and laughed. "No need to respond to that. I was just kidding."

"They kid around too, Mrs. Neeley. We all do. We're normal people."

"People who stand on roofs and wear sunglasses at night."

"Well, yeah, but we have families. We laugh. We spend time together. Just like you Rossis do." He paused and gazed at D.J., who gave him a welcoming smile. "I've been watching. You've got a great family." His gaze shifted to Pop, who did a funny little dance. "A little quirky, maybe, but great. A person can go a long way in life if they have the love and support of their family."

"True."

His words struck me. . .hard. Every bit of progress I'd made in my life—at Club Wed, in my career—could be traced back to two things: my family and my faith. I knew where Agent O'Conner stood on the first, but what about the second?

I'd nearly opened my mouth to broach the subject when Jolene and Bonnie Sue approached.

Jolene shoved a monogrammed napkin in the agent's direction. "It's been so great getting to know you. Could I have your autograph please?"

"Oh, no Ma'am," he said. "I really can't do that. I've never been asked before, but I'm sure it's against policy."

She leaned close and whispered, "I won't tell. Now c'mon, honey. Give me your John Hancock."

O'Conner scribbled the words *Mickey Mouse* onto the napkin and Jolene turned her nose up at them.

"Mickey Mouse?"

He nodded. "Yes, Ma'am. You'll have to take my word for it."

She scurried away, napkin in hand.

"Mickey Mouse?" I laughed. "I know you guys have code names for everything, but. . .really?"

Agent O'Conner shook his head. "He's my son's favorite Disney character. That's all. And if I'd written Donald Duck she might've taken it as an endorsement of one of the candidates." O'Connor slapped himself on the knee. "Sometimes I amaze myself with my humor."

The laughter must've caught D.J.'s attention. He looked up from the soundboard and then walked our way.

"What did I miss?"

"Nothing much," I said. "But O'Conner is voting for Uncle Laz for President."

"Wait. . .you're voting for me?" Laz's voice rang out from my right. "Really? Does that mean you'll protect me when I'm on the campaign trail? If so, I might consider running, after all. Maybe I dropped out too soon!"

"Will you promise to feed me if I do?" O'Conner asked.

"You've got yourself a deal." Uncle Laz extended his hand. "Glad to see you've joined the Rossi team, young man."

"You Rossis *are* quite a team, all right."

Yes, indeed. We were quite a team. And whether Uncle Laz ever saw the inside of the Oval Office or not, I had a feeling we'd go on being a team, no matter what life threw our way.

I slipped my arm around D.J.'s waist and leaned in close as Uncle Laz went off on a tangent about how the world would be different, once he landed in the White House. From across the room I caught a glimpse of Mama and Pop, who'd decided to take to the dance floor. Armando and Scarlet joined them, followed by Nick and Marcella.

"What do you say, Mrs. Neeley?" D.J. asked. "Would you like to take a little spin with me?"

"As long as it's not a *political* spin, I'd love to." I laughed and extended my hand.

My sweetie led me to the dance floor and pulled me into his arms, then kissed me soundly. Mmm. A kiss like that on Valentine's night could put a girl in a romantic frame of mind, no doubt about it. I kissed him back, a long, slow kiss that promised even more, once we arrived home.

Then, with romantic music filling the air, the fella I loved more than life itself swept me off of my feet. . .for the hundred-thousandth time.

Look for More Bella Novellas in 2016!
(Available soon by pre-order)

Once Upon a Moonlight Night
Tea for Two
Pennies from Heaven (A Springtime Garden Ceremony): April 15th 2016:
That Lucky Old Sun (A Galveston Beach Ceremony): July 15th 2016
The Tender Trap (An Autumn Shabby Chic Ceremony): October 15th 2016

Have You Read the Books That Started It All?

THE CLUB WED SERIES:
Fools Rush In
Swinging on a Star
It Had to be You

THE BACKSTAGE PASS SERIES:
Stars Collide
Hello Hollywood
The Director's Cut

THE WEDDINGS BY DESIGN SERIES
Picture Perfect
The Icing on the Cake
The Dream Dress
A Bouquet of Love

ABOUT THE AUTHOR

Award-winning author Janice Thompson got her start in the industry writing screenplays and musical comedies for the stage. Janice has published over 100 books for the Christian market, crossing genre lines to write cozy mysteries, historicals, romances, nonfiction books, devotionals, children's books and more. She particularly enjoys writing light-hearted, comedic tales because she enjoys making readers laugh. Janice is passionate about her faith and does all she can to share the joy of the Lord with others, which is why she particularly enjoys writing. Her tagline, "Love, Laughter, and Happily Ever Afters!" sums up her take on life.

Janice lives in Spring, Texas, where she leads a rich life with her family, a host of writing friends, and two mischievous dachshunds. When she's not busy writing or playing with her eight grandchildren, she can be found in the kitchen, baking specialty cakes and cookies for friends and loved ones. No matter what Janice is cooking up—books, cakes, cookies or mischief—she does her best to keep the Lord at the center of it all. You can find out more about this wacky author at www.janiceathompson.com.

ACKNOWLEDGMENTS

I'm so grateful to the following:

My Dream Team: What an amazing group of readers and friends you are! I could never publish a book without you! (Truly!)

My Cover Designer, Shar (from landofawes): Wow, girl! You have worked so hard on my behalf and I'm grateful, grateful. You truly captured the "Tea for Two" essence in the lovely cover design and I'm tickled pink.

My formatter and friend, Crystal. Love you, girl.

My Private Facebook Indie Group: You guys are the wheels on my bus.

Made in the USA
Middletown, DE
22 February 2016